THE GALVIN
GIRLS

Sophie,

Thank you so much for supporting my book! I hope it brings you as many laughs and smiles while reading it as I experienced while writing it!

all the best,
Emily Schmidt

THE GALVIN GIRLS

A NOVEL

EMILY SCHMIDT

NEW DEGREE PRESS

THE GALVIN GIRLS

A Novel

ISBN   978-1-63676-547-1   *Paperback*

978-1-63676-113-8   *Kindle Ebook*

978-1-63676-114-5   *Ebook*

To Caye, Grace, Kay, and Grandaddy for allowing
me to share the Galvin sisters with the world.

CONTENTS

"But remember, Anna, you being young in years, the responsibility is on you to be as good in the future as you were in the past."

A LETTER FROM CATHERINE DWYER GALVIN
TO HER DAUGHTER, OCTOBER 12, 1933

AUTHOR'S NOTE

———

"I'd like to introduce my granddaughters, Emily and Tara Schmidt. They are dancers with Rince Ri School of Irish Dance," my grandfather said into the microphone.

I grabbed my sister's hand and stood up from the table of young cousins, their encouraging smiles loosening the knot in my stomach. It had been growing for a week since my mom told us we'd be dancing at the party. My grandfather waved us to the wooden dance floor at the head of the banquet hall. Staring into a crowd of mostly unfamiliar faces, I spotted my parents to one side. They gave us a thumbs-up and motioned to smile wider. My socks itched.

My grandfather continued, "Emily joined a summer camp for Irish dancing two years ago. When my mother, Helen, our birthday girl, heard the news, she got up and tried dancing 'Shoe the Donkey' with me. Even in her old age, she can't resist celebrating her great-granddaughter with a jig!"

The ballroom filled with laughter.

"I told her to sit the hell down or she'd break a hip!"

A round of applause and hollers joined the chorus of deafening laughter.

I glanced up from the floor and looked at my great-grandmother Helen. She was absolutely beaming. I thought for sure her dentures would pop out.

My grandfather waved to hush the crowd. "To celebrate Mom's hundredth birthday, my granddaughters will be performing a few Irish jigs to honor our very own Irish rose."

As relative beginners, Tara and I performed every dance we knew well enough. The crowd clapped along to the beat of every tune and cheered at the end of each dance, even when we made mistakes. After a full half-hour performance, I walked off the dance floor toward my parents. My mom immediately ushered me over to my great-grandmother to wish her a happy birthday.

Hunched over in the chair, my great-grandmother reached out and ran her knobby fingers over the intricate Celtic knots embroidered on my orange dance costume.

"Ye danced beautifully," she said, taking my hands in hers.

Her sunken blue eyes were glassy, the irises faded to an almost translucence to match her white curls.

"It brought back memories of when I was a girl, memories locked away for many years."

I squeezed her hands and smiled. She squeezed them back.

I was ten years old when my great-grandmother, Helen Galvin Rush, died a month shy of her hundred and first birthday. Her hundredth birthday party was the last time I danced for her and the last memory I have of her alive.

She was born in Listowel (Lis-TOLL), County Kerry, Ireland in 1908 on a dairy farm. Her parents, Edmond Galvin and Catherine Dwyer Galvin, had a total of fourteen children, twelve of whom lived into adulthood. More than half of her siblings immigrated to the United States during the 1920s, some in their early teenage years and completely alone. They all eventually settled in Philadelphia where most raised their children, including my grandfather and his older brother.

Helen was close with four of her sisters who joined her in Philadelphia: Anna, Mary, Theresa, and Bridie. They lived every single day to the fullest with the opportunities they sought in America. The "Silver Street" they sang about on the journey over became North Bonsall Street, where they rented a two-story row home and lived together at different times before they each got married to the loves of their lives. As incredible as America seemed with its widespread electricity and sprawling department stores, the Galvin sisters never forgot their immigrant identities, especially in the wake of economic tragedy.

I didn't grow up hearing the stories of Helen and her sisters. I knew she had immigrated from Ireland as a teenager and lived in a small rural town whose name I couldn't pronounce, but beyond that, I didn't know anything. She rarely spoke about it. In fact, she didn't visit Listowel again until the late 1970s, nearly twenty years after her parents had passed away. The life she left was too painful to revisit, so she waited until it was gone. My grandfather only knew basic information about his mother's past life in Ireland. He knew it made her sad to talk about it, so he avoided asking about the intimate memories. My own mother, consequently, knew very little, too.

When I read Lalita Tademy's *Cane River*, the somewhat fictionalized story of four generations of Tademy's slavery-born female ancestors, I knew I wanted to dig into my own past, Helen's past. In the summer of 2017, I reached out to my grandfather's cousins, the children of Helen's sisters. I met with two wonderful women, Grace O'Neill and Caye

Haneley, the daughters of Theresa and Mary, and listened to countless stories of struggle, strength, and sisterhood.

In the summer of 2018, my dad and I traveled to Listowel to meet with Kay Scanlon, a first cousin my grandfather never knew existed and the daughter of Josephine Galvin, Helen's youngest sister who chose not to emigrate. She showed us the graves of Helen's parents and siblings, the church where she was baptized, the bar her uncle owned. I visited Ballybunion, the beach she and her sisters frequented in the summer, and Cobh (pronounced "Cove") Harbor, where she and her sisters climbed onto the ships that brought them to America.

Finally, in the summer of 2019, I visited Listowel again, this time with my whole family. My mother met Josephine's daughter, and as I listened to my relatives share stories about the Galvin sisters, I knew I needed to tell their story. As a great-grandchild, I am part of the last generation to have known the last-surviving Galvin who immigrated to Philadelphia. And as the only writer in the family and a sister myself, I believe I can share this story best.

The immigrant tale isn't unique to my great-grandmother and her sisters. Millions of immigrants from all over the world have settled in the US alone, including over two hundred thousand Irish during the 1920s.[1] The story of uprooting one's life to move to another country has been sung in songs, written in diaries, published in books, passed down in families. Irish poet and immigrant Eavan Boland writes in "The Emigrant Irish": "What they survived we could not even live.

---

1   Rebecca Tippett, "US Immigration Flows, 1820-2013," Carolina Demography, April 27, 2015, accessed May 3, 2020; US Department of Homeland Security, *Total Immigrants from each Region and Country, by Decade, 1820–2010,* distributed by Scholastic Corporation.

/ [...] Cardboard. Iron. Their hardships parceled in them. / Patience. Fortitude. Long-suffering / in the bruise-colored dusk of the New World."[2] Every story is stitched with threads of hardship, determination, bravery, and hope—Helen and her sisters' included.

However, one thread is often hidden behind the others when telling these immigrant stories: crisis. Many immigrants choose to leave their homeland because they face a crisis—war, famine, natural disaster, persecution. They look toward their new home with innocent hope for a better life than the one they're leaving behind. And for immigrants coming to the US, that innocent hope is the American Dream. The Galvin sisters all dreamed of lives beyond marrying men from the local Catholic parish, becoming housewives, and raising a dozen children. They wanted independence and opportunity that rural Irish life couldn't offer.

This hope, though, often overlooks the ill-fated possibility of escaping one crisis only to face another. For immigrants who arrived in the US a decade or a year ago, not a single one would have expected the COVID-19 pandemic and resulting economic recession. My great-grandmother and her sisters never imagined enduring the Stock Market Crash of 1929 or the prolonged Great Depression in the 1930s when they immigrated only a few years earlier. None of the 1.6 million immigrants who came between 1920 and 1929 did.[3]

As of July 9, 2020, a staggering 48 million people filed for unemployment for the first time since the beginning of the

2   Eavan Boland, "The Emigrant Irish," Favorite Poem Project, accessed August 16, 2020.

3   US Department of Homeland Security, *Total Immigrants from each Region and Country, by Decade, 1820–2010*, distributed by Scholastic Corporation.

pandemic.[4] Of those 48 million, immigrant workers have faced a steeper employment drop (19 percent) compared to American-born workers (12 percent).[5] While a crisis affects all of us in some way, we forget that people living on the margins—immigrants—tend to struggle even more in the face of a crisis like COVID-19.

My great-grandmother and her sisters lived on the margins of society when the stock market crashed on Black Thursday, October 24, 1929. As young immigrants in economic hardship, they faced the looming uncertainty of their futures in America like many immigrants are confronting at this moment. This novel tells the struggles and victories of five sisters who worked together to survive unexpected crisis. And although *The Galvin Girls* is fictional, the heart of the story is raw and real. It's a story of immigrants overcoming economic hardship and the difficulties of adjusting to life in America, the dark reality of the American Dream.

---

4   "The Impact of COVID-19 on Job Loss: Quick Take," Catalyst, July 22, 2020, accessed August 16, 2020.

5   Rakesh Kochhar, "Hispanic women, immigrants, young adults, those with less education hit hardest by COVID-19 job losses," Pew Research Center, June 9, 2020, accessed August 17, 2020.

PROLOGUE

———

It is late September. I wait in line outside the White Star Line offices, the strong harbor breeze whippin' the curls under me crocheted cloche. I tug it down to protect me dignity from the first- and second-class passengers starin' from the windows above. I stand below them, live below them. I am Anna Galvin, the third-class daughter of a dairy farmer from Listowel. The men, women, and children in this line are third-class people. We will arrive in New York as third-class people. We will live our lives in America, wherever we go, as third-class people. We are immigrants, citizens of the Irish Free State, people of Éire. And yet, I recognize not a single person.

I feel the crumpled ticket inside the pocket of me wool coat. I run me fingers along the multiple creases worn into the paper like the wrinkles on Father's forehead from raisin' his brow. Mother begged me not to lose the ticket.

"It's worth yer life," she said. "Ye can have anythin' ye want with it."

The dilapidated dock ahead looks ready to collapse under the weight of distress present on passengers' faces as they climb into the pair of rowboats. RMS *Cedric* is anchored far off in the harbor, where the breeze becomes a gale that blows the smoke away from the stacks toward Spike Island in the distance. I pull me cloche down further and wrap me coat tighter. Their embrace falls short of Mother's. Father forbade her from seein' me off because she fainted when seein' her eldest son off to England. I told Mary and Helen not to come, for I didn't want to cry.

I look behind me, beyond the tops of baldin' heads and hand-sewn hats to the town Cobh, the jewel of Cork's coast. She is picturesque, the Lord's most perfect artistry. Mother told me I have been here once before to see a neighbor off to England, but I don't remember. Rows of colorful houses sit on the steep hill like a staircase, the roof of one meetin' the door of another. They are wildflowers, clashin' hues and chipped windowpanes, bunches of beauty. The bottom layer, grounded in the main street, consists of family shops, livelihoods, and settled dreams. Their doors are wide open, embracin' customers with music and friendly welcomes. Atop the hill stands St. Colman's Cathedral, watchin' over the harbor. Its steeple pierces the mornin' fog to reach heaven. The bells clang eight times with remorse. I am leavin'. We are leavin'.

The line moves forward, but I am pushed. Me feet do not step ahead. They are planted firmly like a stubborn cow's. Me body lurches, and I crash into the man in front of me. He peers back and nods, an implicit understandin' between us. We are all fearful. I stand upright again, clutchin' me worn, leather luggage, its belted straps ready to break. It contains all the parts of meself. I cannot lose it. I cannot lose meself on this journey. We cannot lose our identities as a good, honest people. We must stay together, whole, sproutin' along the American coast. But we are not weeds; we are cultivated gardens, hard workers, opportunists for beauty. We sail with our dreams of bein' a first-class people.

Me feet move forward now to the front of the line. Me mind stays put in the past—what I leave, who I leave. Me mother and father, me brothers and sisters, me home. I will have a new home. We will all have new homes. We will be Irish in America, never Americans. Our accents mark us. Our devout Catholicism rules us. But our love for music enriches us. And our talent for dance lifts us. I will be Irish in America and American in Ireland upon returnin' one day to visit. I will be a first-class person, self-sufficient and modern. Me independence awaits.

I reach into me pocket and pull out me ticket. It is almost completely torn. I want to rip it, keep one half, but I hand it over, folded, to the ticket collector standin' at the edge of the dock. He puts it in his own pocket. I climb down a ladder and step onto the rowboat without assistance. A man hands me baggage down. I am still a third-class person. Two other women sit next to me. They must be sisters, older with streaks of gray. I look down at their hands clutched together. I clasp me own in prayer but feel no more comfort than holdin' the edge of the bench. The man rowin' pushes off from the dock with one wooden oar. It has several holes in it. The water is choppy, and I bounce in me seat as if ridin' a horse. The sisters draw closer together for support. I grab onto me suitcase. I am me own support, the first Galvin girl in America.

"Not a day will go by when I don't think of ye," Mother said.

"Be the strong farmin' daughter I raised," Father said.

"I'll be followin' close behind ye. It's only a year," Mary said.

"We love ye, Anna," Helen said.

I am scared, but I did not tell them.

The rowboat arrives at the *Cedric*. We are in its loomin' shadow, the American presence. I'm the first to climb up a rope ladder extended from an open door. A burly man in a navy uniform reaches out to help me up. Me luggage is pulled up by a single thick rope. I grab his hand and find me footin' inside. Me hands are red and irritated, four small crescent moons pressed into the center of each palm. The burly man thrusts me baggage into me arms. It feels heavier now. I don't look out the door again.

An older man in a white uniform waves me to follow him. We walk through several narrow hallways and up a long flight of spiral stairs. We step out on the highest deck. Strings of dark flags flutter violently like a merle of blackbirds. The older man ushers me to the edge of the deck, then leaves for the other passengers. I drop me suitcase but do not hear it land. I place me hands on the railin' and look out toward Cobh once again. She is smaller, the colorful houses just specks of paint on a canvas. The air smells of smoke and salt. I can't separate one face from another in the crowd on the shore. The bells still toll, the cryin' much softer from across the harbor. Three deep clangs, twice. A woman's funeral. They will grow silent from across the Atlantic.

CHAPTER 1

BRIDIE'S ARRIVAL

Helen fanned herself with the day's edition of the *Philadelphia Daily News*. Sweat beads gathered along her hairline, ready to fall one at a time like the water ballerinas photographed on the paper's front page. She'd given up reading about the highest stock market peak of the decade after the limp paper stained her hands with ink. Her stockings itched, but she couldn't afford another hole from scratching. Even waiting for the 5:00 p.m. clocker inside Broad Street Station, the early September humidity stretched her dark curls, hiding the clip-on pearl earrings she'd bought herself last Christmas. Her pale pink blouse sagged as if drying on a clothesline. The leather of her T-strap shoes was darkened in spots. Helen continued waving the paper. She hoped the weather would improve with October's coming.

The vaulted ceiling of the train shed offered little respite for people rushing by. Hazy sunbeams shone through the foggy glass at unwanted angles. Men tipped their hats forward and women squinted at the sun as they pushed by each other. The few children Helen spotted had flushed, glistening cheeks. Passenger trains moved in and out of the station, steam hissing and gears squeaking. Every fifteen minutes, a train horn boomed and ricocheted through the station to signal a new arrival. The air around the idle, dark-green locomotives moved in waves with the increasing heat.

Helen's sisters, Mary and Theresa, had promised to meet her by the ticket counter. They usually finished their shifts cutting fabric at the Apex Hosiery factory by four o'clock on Tuesdays, but Helen was sure they would arrive late. Theresa had an awful habit of cooing at every baby that passed by in a carriage. At only seventeen years old, she wanted children more than a husband. Helen was twenty-one and had never held hands with a man other than her father, let alone imagined holding her own child. Mary, just a year older than Helen, often encouraged Theresa's longing for children by talking about the most fashionable American baby names—a terribly irresponsible habit. Helen often reminded them they only kept enough food on the table for themselves, not a mouth more.

Helen had been waiting since half past four, and the train was scheduled to pull in any moment. She heard the weekday evening clockers from New York were almost always full, sometimes overcrowded. She had arrived on a Saturday morning in February 1926. The train car windows rattled the entire two-hour trip. Her wool coat did little to block the whistling wind sneaking through the windowpane next to her seat. She had assured the train conductor her eyes watered only from the consistent frigid breeze, and she had her own handkerchief somewhere. A young girl Helen had seen on the ship kept glancing at her with concern from across the aisle.

The same girl had stood behind her in the medical examination line at Ellis Island. She had watched the doctors examine Helen carefully for defects, abnormalities, or really anything to send her back to Ireland. A part of her wanted them to find something wrong. Each doctor had questioned the ghostly color of her skin and the dark shadows under her gray eyes. The face powder and lipstick her mother had bought as parting gifts did little to hide the exhaustion and seasickness she had endured over the five-day transatlantic journey. Now standing in the train station, Helen imagined that her younger sister, Bridie, had probably faced a similar experience earlier this hot September day. But she doubted Bridie had thought of home once she stepped on the ship.

Anxious about the arrival, Helen had come straight from four o'clock Confession at St. Columba's. At first, she tried walking the several miles to the train station, but when she reached Twenty-Second Street, she gave up and took the trolley the rest of the way. She also knew that swearing in the heat an hour after doing penance was God's way of telling her that paying the trolley fee was worth it.

"Who are you waiting for, ma'am?"

Helen turned away from the bustling scene of trains and people to the ticket counter a few feet behind her. A short, uniformed gentleman stood behind the window, iron bars seeming to imprison him inside the booth. His cracked spectacles sat low on his hook nose. He fixed his crooked necktie as she walked toward him. The man placed his hands atop a neat pile of papers.

"I'm sorry, sir. I couldn't hear ye over the noise. What did ye ask?" Helen said, leaning close to the window.

"Oh yes, it's rather difficult to hear. I inquired who you're waiting for so patiently." The man gestured to the ever-moving crowd in the distance.

Helen didn't normally share her personal business with strangers, but something about this man felt awfully familiar.

She took her pocketbook from the crook of her elbow and laid it on the counter. She unsnapped the fastener, reached inside, and retrieved a small prayer book. A worn photograph fell out and landed facedown. She flipped it over and slid it to the man as if she were paying for a ticket.

"I'm waitin' for me sister, Bridie," Helen said, pointing to the photo now in the man's hands. "She's come all the way from Ireland and passed through Ellis Island today. Me eldest sister, Anna, caught an early clocker this morning to fetch her. The Lord knows Bridie would end up in Boston without Anna's help locatin' the right train to Philadelphia."

The man lifted his spectacles and brought the photo closer to his face. "What a lovely child! Is this photo recent?" he asked.

Helen laughed and shook her head. "No, sir, she's a young woman now—sixteen years old. Me sister Theresa says she has the attitude of a duchess."

"I sure got lucky with only having sons," the man said, handing the photo back to Helen. Then he wiped his shining forehead with a green handkerchief.

She nodded, looking down at the photograph. Her father loved his four Galvin boys. Despite having twelve well-behaved children, he still said that having one son for every two daughters was punishment for a horrific sin he never knew he committed. Her mother always shook her head and said that with an entire dairy farm to run, the best way to find help was to have their own. Boy or girl, every child worked. Helen didn't particularly like getting up before dawn to milk the cows or rake the muck, but she missed hearing her siblings squabble over collecting eggs and climbing the hay bales.

Her chest tightened.

"How long have you been in Philadelphia?"

She hesitated a moment before glancing back up. "About three years now, but it feels much longer."

"I feel nothing ever changes much in this city," the man said, shaking his head. "I moved from New York in '23 to stay with my brother. I hear every day is a party up there with the Harlem boys tooting their horns, even now in '29. Haven't been back since due to the missus. What I wouldn't do to be back in the jazz clubs again."

"I haven't even been back to this station since arrivin'. It's all a bit too much for me, I suppose," Helen said, slipping the photo inside the prayer book.

She looked up at the man again, studying his cartoon-ish features. Where did she know him from? Had he been working at the same booth the day she arrived? Did they have a conversation?

"Let me tell you something, ma'am," he said, interrupting her thoughts. "More Irish live in Philadelphia than Italians live in New York. They should rename the city 'New Ireland.' You can't go a block without bumping into someone speaking the brogue. You should feel more at home here than any other immigrant. And you've got family living with you. Count yourself lucky, ma'am."

"She's blessed with the luck of every saint!"

Mary giggled as she walked up beside Helen and placed an arm around her shoulders. Theresa, holding a bouquet of yellow tulips, stepped to Helen's other side and leaned her head into her sister's shoulder for a few seconds. Helen looked up to Mary then down to Theresa like a trio of nesting dolls lined up. Dark curls, light eyes, pale skin of varying similitude. Mary resembled their father with thick brows and gangling limbs. Her hair peeked out beneath her cloche like freshly sheared black wool, with or without the humidity.

Theresa had a china doll's features and a child's stature. She claimed placing folded handkerchiefs in the heels of her shoes would bring her closer to the kingdom of heaven.

"Good golly, no one can mistake the resemblance between you ladies," the man said, moving his spectacles up his nose.

"Just wait until our other sisters step off the train, sir!" Theresa's words bounced like the tune of a jig. Usually more soft-spoken, she mimicked Mary's unabashed excitement.

Helen turned her back to the ticket counter and pulled her sisters into a circle. She looked at the tulips under Theresa's right arm, inhaled the hot air, and sighed, her whole frame rising and falling. It was five past five, and had the train arrived on time, they would've missed it—all for flowers that wilted in a day.

"What took ye so long to get here?"

"We started chattin' with a lovely woman sellin' tulips just outside O'Hara's Beauty Parlor," Mary said. "She grew the flowers in pots on the back steps of her home. I'd never imagine any plant growin' in this horrid heat!"

Theresa glanced at Mary and nodded. "It's positively dreadful outside. I can't go anywhere without stainin' the back of me dress. It's like I'm a child again, soilin' all me clothes."

"If ye hadn't stopped to talk in the sun for so long, ye wouldn't be sweatin' so much. And since when do ye care about yer appearance, Theresa?" Helen said, putting a hand on her hip. Sometimes the two of them together made her consider returning to Ireland to escape their frivolity.

"Oh, Helen, aren't the tulips just so beautiful and vibrant?" Mary asked. She pulled a tulip from the bouquet, broke off the bottom half of the stem, and placed it behind Helen's ear.

Ignoring Helen's comment, Theresa grinned and clapped her palms in quick succession. "The yellow pairs so nicely with her blouse. Don't ye agree, Mary?"

"I always said yellow was her color. A pretty pale yellow like a newborn ducklin'—"

"Or me skin when I kept cookin' and eatin' sweet potatoes for dinner every day last November," Helen said, taking the tulip out of her hair.

Theresa dropped the bouquet and bent over in a fit of giggles. Mary shrieked and threw her hands up. Helen couldn't hear their cacophony of laughs above the evening hubbub of the train station, but the tears they both wiped away indicated she had won the silly argument. Pale yellow wasn't and would never be her color.

"Will ye two refrain from embarrassin' yerselves in a public place, please?" Helen asked, turning back to the ticket counter to hide her smile. Some of the squabbling she dearly missed had followed her to America.

The man had nodded off, so she cleared her throat. He opened his eyes and blinked several times before realizing he had fallen asleep on the job. He straightened his tie, then folded his hands on the pile of papers again. She had seen him before in this exact spot where she had waited for Anna and Mary to take her home. They had been late to her arrival.

"How may I help you, ma'am?"

"What track does the 5:00 p.m. clocker come in on?"

"Track three. Just turn around and walk straight back. There's a sign above the end point."

"Have a lovely evenin', sir."

Helen waved to the man and spun back to her sisters. Theresa had picked up the bouquet, but a few petals still lay on the tiled floor. She carefully arranged the tulips in one hand while Mary fanned the front of her legs with her skirt as if shaking out a dusty quilt. The evening's golden sunbeams glinted through the train shed's dirt-speckled windows and cast a shadow on her sisters' profiles, lighting up the frizz framing their faces. Helen stepped forward and held up her left hand to block the rays.

"Where do we have to go?" Mary asked, continuing to fan her skirt.

Helen pointed to the back of the station. "They're arrivin' on the third track."

"I think that's the same track me train came on last summer," Theresa said as she switched the bouquet from one arm to the other.

"And mine as well," Mary agreed.

A train horn echoed from down the track. Fifteen minutes past the hour, the 5:00 p.m. clocker rolled into the station, steam puffs rising to the ceiling. Helen felt the vibrations of the train's forward motion and sudden halt under her feet. She walked ahead of her sisters toward the track, her pocketbook hitting her hip with every stride. Mary and Theresa called behind her, but she kept weaving through the crowd. The passenger car doors opened, and the train conductors stepped out, assisting the first passengers down the stairs. Helen picked up her pace, her heels clicking against the tiled floor like a horse trot on cobblestone. Her eyes stayed fixed on the last passenger car.

She stopped a trolley's length away and waited. Mary and Theresa caught up with her a moment later, breathing heavily from pushing and shoving through the crowd. Just as Helen reached for her sisters' hands, she spotted a familiar blue hat amid the passengers moving away from the train.

"All the Galvin girls arrive on track three," she whispered.

CHAPTER 2

THE LOCKET

———

"Bridie! Anna! We're over here!" Helen called, waving a hand above her head.

Spotting the three sisters through the crowd, Anna grinned and waved back. She grabbed Bridie's free hand and led her around others congregating near the track and waiting to meet their loved ones. Bridie's facial features blurred as tears formed in Helen's eyes. She hadn't seen or written to her younger sister in three years. Anna and Theresa primarily sent the letters home to their mother for news of Listowel and family recipes. Helen tried to write, but each time she threw her unfinished letter into the fireplace, whether it was lit or not.

Mary and Theresa ran to meet Anna and Bridie with open arms. Helen stayed put and watched her sisters embrace with more joy than a mother holding her newborn child for the first time. A couple tears rolled down her cheeks. Bridie was finally home—a home Helen still hadn't fully accepted. From Bridie's awe in gazing around the train station, Helen knew her younger sister would never see Listowel as home again. Helen looked down at her shoes. Another tear fell onto her right toe. The joy and excitement she had anticipated feeling only transformed into a disquieted ache in her chest. Her vision blurred even more. Glancing up at the enormous clock above the ticket counter, she couldn't read the position of the minute hand.

The train shed suffocated her like the third-class ship cabin she had slept in on the journey over. She needed to get out. This was the reason she hadn't come with Anna and Mary to pick up Theresa last year. She looked back to her sisters, now conversing with dramatic hand gestures. Anna caught her eye and waved her over, but Helen shook her head and rushed toward the train station's main door. Her head throbbed with a raw nostalgia she'd managed to bridle to a numbness since the day she arrived.

Helen pushed open the door with both hands and stepped onto Broad Street. The afternoon's intense heat had subsided enough that she could take a deep breath without feeling fatigued, though it shook like a stubborn motorcar engine. She squinted as the sun peeked out from behind City Hall and underneath the station's roofed arcade. To her left and right, people streamed out of all the station's entrances onto the sidewalk. Some dodged the cars and crossed onto Market Street, while others walked up and down Broad Street. A group of men next to her huddled over an open newspaper, arguing over who would buy the most stocks by morning.

Being in Center City on a weekday evening reminded Helen of her trip to Dublin with her mother before she left for America. The cities shared a constant movement of vehicles—bicycles, automobiles, trolleys, double-deck buses. Crossing the street was almost impossible without a honk or yell from drivers, even when police directed traffic and waved on pedestrians. However, Dublin's chatter was much louder with the number of pubs that lined the central streets. Any hour of the day, lively ceili music and the slurred singing of drunken men drifted out the propped doors and lured in those looking for a good time. In Philadelphia, she rarely heard anything above the motors but the high-pitched calls of young paper boys looking to sell the day's breaking news. This was supposed to be her home now.

"Ye could've held the door for us," Mary said as she caught the door just before it shut.

Helen turned away from the street and grabbed the door's brass handle. It burned her hand enough that she loosened her grip to just her fingertips, but she didn't want to let it go again. Mary and Anna exited in single file, but she had to open the door wider so Theresa and Bridie could pass through as a pair with their arms linked. They each held a handful of tulips in their free arms.

"I didn't realize ye were that far behind me," Helen said, letting the door close on its own.

"Ye made an escape without tellin' us," Anna said while ushering Theresa and Bridie away from the door to avoid blocking others from coming in and out.

Helen brushed away perspiration near her right temple and followed Anna. "I was feelin' a bit light-headed from the heat, but I'm just fine now."

"I was close to faintin' meself while workin' today. Me hands were sweatin' so much that the scissors kept slippin' while cuttin' fabric. Me count for the day was lower than normal," Mary said, taking her straw cloche off to smooth her curls.

Anna grimaced. "It's a shame ye don't work near an open window. I think Mr. Henry should start rotatin' women around the floor since ye're all doin' the same job."

Mary placed her cloche back down and brushed the stray hair away from her eyes. "I'm mighty surprised no others have fainted yet. This heat has lasted since the first of September, and now it's the ninth. I think an ice bath is in order when we arrive home."

Anna leaned over and squeezed Mary's left shoulder. "And where are ye goin' to get the ice?" she asked.

"I was hopin' ye'd know!"

"In this heat, I know where to get melted ice," Anna said, her penciled eyebrows raised.

Helen glanced between Anna and Mary. As the eldest sister at twenty-four, Anna naturally assumed the role of their mother figure. She looked the part, too. Thin wisps of gray covered her dark curls like a cobweb. She refused to pull them out because two hairs always grew back in the place of one. Over the summer, she carried an umbrella wherever she went to prevent the sun from darkening her skin. She wasn't a farmer's daughter in America. Today, Anna wore her Tre-Jur lipstick in "Radiant Red," her favorite among the six shades of red she owned. She saved it for special occasions because it was nearly double the price of the other reds.

Mary sighed and fanned her legs again. "I suppose a normal bath will do, although Bridie needs a good scrubbin' the most. Travelin' such a long way always leaves a coatin' of dirt in the places ye least expect."

Helen remembered the grease and grime that had collected in her stockings and shoes when she came on the boat to America. It took two whole bars of soap and several baths to feel completely clean. She looked over at Bridie, who was nodding along to Theresa's story. Her youngest sister's hair had turned from brown to auburn since she'd last seen her. It was plaited and pinned, not a single hair astray despite the long trip and awful humidity. Freckles sprinkled the bridge of her nose and upper cheeks. As a child, Helen had convinced herself and her other siblings that Bridie was part fairy with her prominent cheekbones and upturned eyes. Theresa even thought Bridie was a changeling because she fussed more than all the sisters combined.

"How are we gettin' back to Bonsall Street?" Theresa asked over her shoulder.

Mary looked to Anna for an answer, but Helen kept her eyes on Bridie. Her sister stared at the ground and fiddled with a gold locket necklace she didn't recognize.

"I thought we'd take the trolley back home. I believe one's leavin' in fifteen minutes just around the corner," Mary said.

Anna nodded in agreement. "It's rather hot to walk several miles home. I'm sure Bridie's exhausted and wants to lay down for the rest of the evenin'."

"I think we should walk at least part of the way," Helen said, switching her pocketbook from one arm to the other. "It's her first time in Philadelphia. She should see part of Twenty-Second Street with all the local shops we love, and then we can catch a trolley from there. It's only a twenty-minute walk."

Anna and Mary exchanged a look of uncertainty. Helen knew they were all drained from the long day, but she wanted Bridie to see the city. From the news Anna received in their mother's letters, Bridie had never been to Dublin or even Cork. The busy urban environment would most certainly be an adjustment from her quiet farm life. It still was for Helen.

"I suppose it's gettin' later in the evenin' now," Anna said, the first few words strung together in one breath. "Bridie, what do ye think about seein' the city?"

"I've got a terrible headache, but I'll do whatever Helen wants. It doesn't matter."

Just a few minutes earlier, Bridie had been chatting away like a middle-aged widow in the church courtyard after Mass. Her indifference seemed sudden and without reason besides the heat. Of course, Helen couldn't make any judgments because she had been rather cross after her long journey, too. Bridie's flushed cheeks concealed most of the lighter freckles below her eyes. She hunched her shoulders enough that she appeared shorter than Theresa. Anna probably thought she looked terrible. Proper posture denoted proper manners according to Mrs. *Smith's Guide to Social Etiquette*, the most important book, second only to the Holy Bible, in Anna's opinion.

Helen opened her mouth to concede her proposed plan, but then she remembered how her first walk through the city three years before had temporarily dissolved her own melancholy. Along Twenty-Second Street, untouched snow had blanketed rooftops and glittered when the weak February sun emerged from behind the clouds. Dozens of footprint trails intersected along the storefronts and crossed in the sloshy streets. Anna and Mary had walked ahead of her, pointing out local favorites and greeting neighbors who passed. Her breath had spread through the stiff air like a puff of cigarette smoke after escaping through her mouth. While her fingers and toes were numb, Helen tingled with the wonder and awe of the Holy Ghost.

If Bridie still resisted going to Mass every Sunday like she had as a child, Helen guessed she didn't pray at all during the trip. All the sisters admitted a strong faith was integral to enduring the physical and emotional trials of immigration, an economic pilgrimage. Helen wanted Bridie to have her same experience, one that transforms loneliness into curiosity and excitement by the power of the Lord, but for longer than the duration of the walk to her new home.

"I promise ye will start feelin' better on the stroll. We'll walk on the shady side of the street," Helen said, picking up her sister's faded leather luggage. It was much lighter than she expected.

Looking both directions before stepping off the sidewalk, she shepherded her sisters across the street. Like they had stood under the arcade, Mary and Anna joined Helen, and the two youngest followed several feet behind in silence. The older sisters walked at a leisurely pace, but fast enough that for every two strides Helen and Anna took, Mary took only one. Bridie and Theresa fell behind quickly, and strangers filled in the space separating the two groups.

"How was the train ride down?" Mary asked, her voice low enough for only Anna and Helen to hear.

Anna looked over her shoulder at Theresa and Bridie trailing even further, then said, "We didn't talk for most of the trip. I tried askin' her about the ship and Ellis Island, but she gave only vague answers. When I tried to pry more, she said she was too tired to talk."

Helen swung Bridie's suitcase in front of her as they passed a group of businessmen on the left. She felt nothing shift around with the sharp movement, so she shook it up and down. Nothing discernible.

"I'm rather surprised. She was always a garrulous child. Remember when she led the supper prayer once and asked the Lord for twelve puppies and named all of 'em? Mother tried to shush her after six, but she kept goin'," Mary said, crow's feet appearing around her eyes.

"I know. That's what I was thinkin'. She said the journey was uneventful other than she got seasick a couple times, and she didn't get stopped for any reason in the medical examination."

Mary began, "I believe the medical examination because she appears healthier than any of us—"

"If I passed through lookin' like a beggar child in stolen clothin', she must be tellin' the truth," Helen chimed in.

"—and can sway any man with a battin' of those long eyelashes."

"And the Lord knows it will get her in trouble soon enough," Anna said, shaking her head.

Helen shook the luggage once more, this time with more vigor. She didn't expect to hear anything if Bridie had only packed clothing, but she felt nothing shift around. For a young girl who used to carry and play with department store catalogs like dolls, she sure didn't pack much clothing for a permanent move to America. Helen also knew their mother wouldn't let any of her daughters leave without packing a brand-new outfit, including a hat and a pair of shoes. She peeked back at Bridie to get a second look at the gold necklace she noticed earlier. The locket was hidden beneath Bridie's dress collar, but the thin chain glinted in the sunbeams that extended between multistory buildings.

"Did either of ye notice Bridie's necklace?" Helen asked.

Mary furrowed her eyebrows.

"I do believe she was fiddlin' with a necklace for most of the train ride. I can't remember what it looked like, though," Anna said.

Helen nodded. "I noticed it at the train station. It's a gold locket, but from what I could see, it looked rather expensive."

"How can ye be so sure?" Mary asked, slowing her pace to match Helen's.

"I believe the locket had a green gemstone, maybe an emerald."

Anna let out a quiet gasp. "An emerald? Do ye know how much that necklace would cost? If Mother ever bought a necklace that valuable, she'd never give it away."

Holding out Bridie's suitcase toward Mary, Helen said, "Feel the weight of Bridie's luggage. I've been tryin' to determine how much is in here, but I'm not sure it's anythin' at all."

Mary grabbed the handle and brought the bag to her side. She lifted it up and down as Helen had done, then passed it to her other hand and repeated the motion.

"I haven't the slightest idea what's in here," she said, giving it back to Helen.

"I know a way of learnin' without openin' it ourselves," Anna said. She bit the right side of her lip and peeked over her shoulder again to make sure Bridie and Theresa hadn't caught up without her noticing.

Helen and Mary both looked at Anna and raised their eyebrows. She was rarely one to come up with an underhanded plan. Helen, on the other hand, was surreptitious. Anna often ruined her well-planned investigations at the expense of propriety. Just last week, Theresa had returned home from the cinema with a few girls from St. Columba's much later than she'd promised. Helen suspected she hadn't gone with friends at all. Theresa seemed sweet on an Italian boy she had met while shopping with Helen at H. Wall's Grocery. She spied them having a conversation but couldn't overhear it from the produce section. When Theresa went out again to the cinema the next night, Helen planned to follow her. Anna caught her sneaking out just after Theresa and threatened to drag her all the way to Confession that minute.

"What do ye propose?" Mary asked, the sincerity in her voice wavering.

Anna tilted her head and rolled her eyes at her younger sister. "I promise it's foolproof. Like ye said, Bridie's goin' to need a bath. While ye and Helen draw it for her, I'll offer to take the bag up to her room. Then, I'll sneak a peek without her knowin' nothin' at all."

"She might object to yer takin' her luggage," Helen said.

"She'll be much too tired," Anna insisted, looking toward Mary for agreement.

Mary shrugged, then skipped forward and twirled in a circle. Her skirt fluttered high enough for men to spot her silk peach bloomers and whistle as they passed in the opposite direction. Anna shook her head and stared at the ground, trying to hide a slight smile. Helen laughed at her older sister's carefree attitude. She understood why Mary's beau, Jimmy Higgins, considered her a handful at times. Though lively himself, he'd put up with her antics for the past year and a half without wincing once. The sisters absolutely adored him and his propensity to bring them all flowers from time to time.

"We're just comin' up on me favorite clothin' shops," Mary said, pointing at the colorful hats in the first shop's display window.

Anna, chuckling, slapped Mary's hand down in jest. "Ye have enough hats to gift every woman at St. Columba's with three each!"

Mary stopped walking and gaped at her sister. "And how many red lipsticks do ye have?" she asked, placing a hand on her hip.

"Many fewer than yer number of hats, may I remind ye—"

"We should take a quick stop inside and introduce Bridie to Mrs. Lynn," Helen said to halt the escalation of a shallow quarrel that had occurred twice earlier in the week.

Anna clasped her hands together in delight. "Oh! That's a wonderful idea, Helen," she said. All traces of pettiness vanished from her voice.

"I couldn't agree more," Mary said, spinning around and grabbing Helen and Anna's hands. She pulled them through the crowd back toward their younger sisters. Helen apologized left and right as she bumped into people. She also rammed the suitcase into a leg or two.

"How far back did they get?" Anna asked, still dodging oncoming people.

"I thought they were only a short—"

"Anna! Mary! Helen!" Theresa shouted.

Helen broke free from Mary's tight grip and pushed straight ahead. The crowd grew thinner as she ran down the sidewalk. The suitcase seemed heavier than it had earlier. She looked behind to see her sisters in close pursuit. Up ahead, she spotted a small group huddled around someone lying on the ground, her legs sprawled widely. When Helen reached the group, she dropped the suitcase and shoved gawking bystanders aside.

There lay Bridie, unconscious with her head bleeding and the gold locket in her open palm.

CHAPTER 3

BRIDIE TELLS
THE TRUTH

———

"Where am I?"

Bridie's soft voice startled Helen out of prayer. She looked up from the tangled rosary beads in her lap to see her younger sister finally awake. The Lord had answered her most desperate plea. She'd never let a cuss word slip from her lips again for as long as she lived. She would be a paragon of holiness. The tightness in her chest settled a little. She stood from the upholstered armchair next to the bed, still holding the rosary beads in one hand, and picked up a damp washcloth from the bedside table.

"Bridie, ye're … home. In Anna and Mary's bedroom," Helen said, placing the washcloth on her sister's forehead. It was lopsided to avoid the open gash.

"Home?"

Helen smiled softly and dabbed the washcloth. "Yes, yer new home in America."

"How did I get here?"

"A couple of kind men stopped to help when they saw ye hurt and offered to drive us home."

Bridie blinked several times, scrunching her nose. "I don't understand—"

"Ye're awake!" Theresa gasped as she walked through the door with a fresh bowl of warm water. She dropped it on the hardwood floor at the foot of the bed, making Helen jump, then crawled under the blanket next to Bridie. Helen bent over and dried the resulting puddle with the edge of her skirt. Theresa wasn't normally this careless, but Anna would most certainly fuss about someone slipping and getting a gash to match Bridie's.

"What happened to the locket?"

Helen stood up on her knees, placing her hands on the bed. She didn't think Bridie would notice the locket's absence so quickly. Theresa turned away from Bridie touching her bare neck and locked eyes with Helen.

"Where's the locket? What happened?"

Theresa shook her head ever so slightly. Only Helen could see the movement.

Helen glanced away from Theresa and smiled at Bridie. "Don't ye worry about the locket. We're waitin' for Anna and Mary to come back with Dr. Burns. Ye took a mighty fall on the way home from the train station and hit yer head."

Bridie moved the washcloth on her forehead and winced when it brushed against the wound. It started bleeding again, so Helen grabbed a dry rag from the linen drawer in her sisters' wardrobe opposite the foot of the bed. Mary had a habit of collecting fabric scraps from the factory at the end of each workweek. She insisted no fabric should go to waste—stained, torn, or hideous. Reusing fabric was better than buying it new. Helen always thought this particular habit was strange for a woman who refused to purchase hats secondhand.

She walked around the other side of the bed and held the rag on the gash. Helen felt like her mother tending to her child's injury, but she couldn't remember the hymn her mother always hummed. Blood soaked through, so she took a few more fabric scraps and layered them, adding more pressure. The song still didn't come. Bridie shut her eyes, her eyebrows knitting together. The blood seeped through again.

"She's goin' to need medical dressin'," Theresa said, pulling back the quilt and hopping off the bed. She took the entire pile of fabric scraps from the drawer and laid it next to Bridie's pillow.

"It looks like you're more than prepared," Dr. Burns announced as he ducked under the bedroom's doorframe.

The middle-aged doctor was taller than any man Helen had ever seen. He wore a tan suit with dark brown Oxfords and carried a worn black leather bag. His green eyes were too close together for Helen's taste, but his trimmed mustache resembled her Grandfather Mortimer's. Dr. Burns still had a full head of hair, but she was convinced he rubbed shoe polish in places to hide the gray.

Just before Helen arrived in America, Mary had caught scarlet fever and worsened by the hour. Anna didn't know where to find a doctor, so she knocked on every neighbor's door up and down Bonsall Street in the middle of the night. On the fourth try, she found Dr. Burns tending to his ill baby. When Anna realized his youngest child also had the fever, she begged him to stay at home, but he insisted on seeing Mary's condition. He went back and forth between Mary and his baby, checking on them until both fevers broke by dawn. If one person could take care of Bridie's wound, he could.

Anna entered the bedroom right after Dr. Burns and fell to her knees when she realized Bridie had woken up. She made the sign of the cross and bowed her head in silent prayer. Mary walked in, focused on searching for something in her pocketbook, and tripped over Anna's feet. Dr. Burns caught her before she hit the floor, but the contents of her pocketbook spilled everywhere—used handkerchiefs, two tubes of lipstick, at least a dozen hairpins, and Bridie's golden locket. Helen shook her head and sighed. Mary pushed the doctor away and scrambled to pick up the belongings and place them back in her bag. Anna stayed deep in prayer.

Dr. Burns chuckled as Mary stood up and straightened her hat. "That was quite the big entrance, Miss Mary."

"She's always stealin' the spotlight," Anna said, making the sign of the cross again.

Mary stepped over Anna's legs and walked over to Helen. "Well, I wasn't the one droppin' to the floor like the Lord himself had come again."

Dr. Burns extended a hand to Anna to help her up. "At least I was thankin' the Lord for lettin' our sister live, and ye're worried about gettin' her a proper gift."

"The Lord told me she was goin' to be just fine, so I was thinkin' ahead," Mary said, looking over at Bridie. "He's always tellin' me things first, ye know."

"Why don't we all turn our attention to the patient in need," Dr. Burns said, placing his bag down on the bed.

Helen nodded and stepped back to give the doctor room next to Bridie. He opened his bag and took out a stethoscope.

Theresa shyly pointed to the mound of fabric scraps. "Excuse me, Doctor...I think ye can see she's bleedin' from the head—"

"Let the man do his job. He performs miracles, right, Mary?" Anna said, moving behind Theresa and wrapping one arm around her.

Dr. Burns smiled as he listened to Bridie's chest. "Give me a deep breath in...now a deep breath out."

"Does everythin' sound like it's workin'?" Bridie asked. She tried to shift into a higher sitting position, but Dr. Burns stopped her.

"Don't move right now. From the looks of it, you hit your head pretty hard and might get dizzy from sitting up too tall."

"The room is spinnin', now that ye mention it."

Dr. Burns held up one finger in front of Bridie. "Please follow my finger and tell me if the number of fingers increases."

This was the first real medical examination, aside from the prodding at Ellis Island, that Helen had ever seen. She didn't understand why Bridie needed to follow and count fingers. Her forehead had bled through numerous rags and Dr. Burns was focused on testing her vision. When Anna fell off a hay bale as a child, Helen remembered the county doctor from Tralee staying no more than five minutes to examine her older sister's swollen ankle. He just instructed her to stay in bed and drink warm water with crushed rosemary to help with the pain.

"Your vision seems normal, so let's take a look at that wound on your forehead." Dr. Burns lifted the multiple layers of rags.

Crusty, dried blood framed the edges of the wound. The entire right side of Bridie's forehead had begun to swell, purple and blue bruises alternating around the gash. Helen's stomach gurgled and her throat tightened, so she forced herself to look away. Whenever her father slaughtered a pig or goat, she always ran to the farthest corner of the property to overcome her wooziness. Mary grabbed her hand and gave it a light squeeze. Helen returned two squeezes.

"It doesn't look deep, but you have lost a good amount of blood. I'll definitely have to sew it up to avoid further excessive bleeding."

Helen looked back in shock. Fear replaced queasiness when she realized Dr. Burns needed to sew up Bridie's wound like Anna did with stockings in the factory.

"Is it goin' to hurt?" Bridie asked, curling up her legs under the blanket.

Dr. Burns shook his head as he reached into his bag. "Probably not more than the fall."

Bridie looked around at her sisters and stopped on Theresa. "I remember walkin' with ye, but I don't remember fallin'. What happened to me locket?"

"It's normal to not remember. Do you remember everything leading up to the fall?" Dr. Burns asked, opening a bottle of antiseptic.

"Yes, I was walkin' home from the train station after Anna and I arrived from New York. I was feelin' rather unsteady in the heat. Theresa and I had fallen behind the others."

"Good, your long-term memory sounds just fine. It may take some time to remember what happened right before the fall. You seem to have hit your head pretty hard."

Dr. Burns picked up a rag from the pile on the bed and wet it with the antiseptic. Then he dabbed the outer edges of the wound and wrung out the remaining liquid into the gash itself. Bridie squeezed the blanket until her knuckles turned white. He opened a jar of long sewing needles and removed one. While dipping it into the bottle of antiseptic, he reached out and patted her hand.

"You don't want to lose too much blood now," Dr. Burns said, winking.

All the sisters let out the same nervous laugh, the sort their mother used to ask if their womanly blood had finally arrived.

Bridie pulled her hand away and bit her lip. "I have enough blood in me body to lose a little more."

After a moment, Dr. Burns removed the needle from the bottle and threaded it. Bridie's body visibly shook. Pinching the edges of the wound together, he stuck the needle through the skin and pulled the black thread through. Bridie clenched her teeth as a few tears slid down her cheeks. He slowly continued the process of pinching, poking, and pulling, only stopping to soak up blood dripping down Bridie's forehead. With each movement, she shut her eyes tighter and inhaled sharply. When he finished the last stitch, Helen squeezed Mary's hand once more. Mary returned two squeezes.

Dr. Burns dabbed some additional antiseptic around the closed wound to remove dried blood. He pulled gauze from his bag and unwound it to wrap it around Bridie's head, tucking in the end to secure it.

All things bright and beautiful, all creatures great and small. Helen sighed. Her mother's song wasn't lost to her.

"Not too terrible, right, Miss Bridie?"

"I've experienced worse pain," Bridie said, touching the soft bandage.

Anna tilted her head and placed a hand on her hip. "And when was that?" she asked, trying not to laugh.

"Well, I suppose it was more of an embarrassin' pain than a physical one when that wretched Grady O'Leary cut off me braids five summers ago for me sayin' he was uglier than his prize-winnin' hog."

Helen's jaw dropped. She remembered the day when Bridie had walked home from town wearing a knitted cap she'd never seen before. It was also an unusually hot summer day. When she asked where the hat had come from, Bridie said it was a gift, and she had to wear it for societal acceptance. Helen didn't think much about her sister's tendency for being dramatic. Their mother, however, eyed the cap all through supper and eventually demanded it come off. Bridie's long braids had been cut jaggedly just below her chin. She claimed that Helen had dared her to try a new hairstyle. After that supper, they didn't talk for an entire week.

"I wouldn't doubt you in the least. My daughters adore their hair," Dr. Burns said, placing the medical supplies back in his bag.

Anna picked up the pile of fabric scraps from the bed and placed them back in the open linen drawer. She then stepped next to the doorframe and watched Dr. Burns fasten his bag. "When will ye be visitin' again to check up on her?"

"I'll be back tomorrow to see how it's healed and make sure an infection hasn't formed."

"Thank ye very much, Doctor. I'll see ye to the front door downstairs," Anna said, letting Dr. Burns exit first. She closed the bedroom door behind her a little too hard. The four porcelain crosses, one hanging on each wall, shook.

"Now that it seems I'm just fine, will ye please tell me what happened to me locket?" Bridie asked.

Theresa sat back down on the bed next to Bridie. "Someone tried to snatch it from yer neck."

Bridie glanced from Theresa to Mary to Helen, her eyebrows furrowed. "Who?"

Theresa sighed and tucked a curl behind her ear. "It all happened so quickly. We were walkin' pretty slowly, and a group of good-lookin' fellas was approachin' from the other direction. The one leadin' called out some rather immodest compliments about ye, but ye ignored him. When he realized ye weren't takin' to him, he reached out and tried to grab yer necklace as he passed. Ye must've saw him comin' and grabbed the necklace yerself before he could. When he failed to get the necklace, he pushed ye from the side and ran off laughin' with the others. Ye fell into me and hit yer head on the ground. When I turned ye on yer back, the necklace was in yer hand."

"So, the locket is safe?"

"Yes, but the clasp is broken," Mary said, opening her purse and taking out the locket. She stepped past Helen and gave it to Bridie.

She played with the golden chain in her hands, examining the green gemstone closely. "Did ye get a good look at the man who pushed me?"

Theresa stared up at the ceiling for a moment, then looked at Bridie. "He wasn't particularly different lookin' than any other fella, but all the men in the group wore the same belt—brown leather with a vertical red stripe on either side of the buckle. I've never seen anythin' like it."

Helen didn't understand how Theresa noticed such a minute detail. Her children would be the most behaved in all of Philadelphia with her sister's close eye. She wondered if Theresa had seen the insert in yesterday's paper about children joining the city's gangs younger and younger each year. The matching belts...those men must've been part of a gang. Helen used to see bands of farm boys marching in matching uniforms around like the Irish Republican Army, but none of them ever hurt anyone. She needed to find that paper again.

Bridie nodded, still turning the locket over in her hands.

"Where did the locket come from?" Helen asked, stepping toward the bed.

"I—I got it from a friend—on the ship."

Helen crossed her arms. "What was the friend's name? Where's she from?"

"Her name was Patricia, and I think she's from Mallow."

Mary sat down on the edge of the bed. "What kind of gemstone is on the locket?"

"It's an emerald."

Helen and Mary looked at each other, then back at Bridie.

"I promise it's real."

"And why did Patricia give ye a gold locket with a real emerald?" Theresa asked.

"Is it because ye traded all yer new clothin' and shoes?"

Anna stood in the doorway holding Bridie's empty luggage. Nothing was in it but a few pieces of paper and a pair of nude stockings. Unusually light for a transatlantic trip.

"Bridie, what happened to the clothin' Mother bought ye before comin'? She wrote me all about it, so don't deny her buyin' ye new dresses from the catalog," Anna said, placing the suitcase on the floor.

Bridie bit her lip and looked around at her sisters. Helen uncrossed her arms and joined Theresa and Mary on the bed. She wasn't the least bit surprised. Bridie had always begged for the prettiest trinkets in the shop windows all around the square. Helen reached out and took Bridie's hand.

"We're not angry with ye. We just want to know what happened, especially with ye gettin' hurt," Mary said.

A few tears rolled down Bridie's cheeks. "I traded me clothin' for Patricia's necklace because I wanted to look rich in America."

"Why would Patricia trade ye an emerald necklace for some clothin'?" Anna asked.

"I told her the clothin' was really expensive and she somehow believed me."

Helen wiped away Bridie's tears with her thumb. "Why would ye want to look rich comin' here?"

"So I didn't look like an Irish immigrant farm girl."

Shaking her head, Anna said, "None of us wanted to look like immigrants after passin' through Ellis Island."

"Mother and Father sent us to make a new life and earn our own way in the world," Mary added.

"We all like buyin' nice things. Anna and Mary have more lipsticks and hats than any woman at St. Columba's." Helen laughed. "We just work hard to buy them, and ye're goin' to work, too."

Bridie's shoulders slumped.

Anna raised her chin and looked down at Bridie. "There's no barterin' and lyin' in me house. Ye can work at the hosiery factory like the rest of us."

"I'm not workin' in a factory. I'll just go to the pawn shop, sell the necklace, and save the money for the future."

Helen patted her sister's hand. "Are ye still decent at stylin' and cuttin' hair?"

Bridie smiled, her dimples appearing. "I did Erin McDowell's hair for her weddin' this spring, if that means anythin'."

"I know a woman who works at O'Hara's Beauty Parlor. I will ask about an assistant position," Helen said. She knew Bridie needed to work to make ends meet with another mouth to feed, but she wanted her younger sister to see America as she had hoped. A country where anything was possible.

"I guess that's better than workin' in a factory—"

"Only if ye like hearin' about the gossip of high society American women," Anna said, winking.

Mary stood up from the bed and put the strap of her pocketbook over her shoulder. The cuckoo clock downstairs chimed seven times.

"Where are ye goin' at this hour?" Helen asked, looking out the window at the setting sun.

"I hate to leave all of ye, but I have to meet Jimmy in the park. He says he's got a big surprise!"

"Well, we're not keepin' ye here. Go and tell him we say hello!" Anna said, shooing Mary out of the bedroom.

"Who's this Jimmy?" Bridie asked, removing her hand from Helen's to scratch her leg.

Helen cleared her throat. "The man who better be makin' a Galvin girl his wife."

"And if it's not Mary, it'll be me," Anna said, wiggling her eyebrows.

"Does he make a high wage?" Bridie sat up straighter and folded her hands on top of the blanket.

Anna crossed her arms. "And why would that matter?"

"If he wants to impress his new future sister-in-law, he'd be smart to come bearin' gifts when he visits."

Helen looked at Theresa and rolled her eyes. She needed to talk to Mira Jameson at O'Hara's immediately. Their mother had warned Anna in her letters that Bridie was a crow attracted to shiny objects. Helen intended for Bridie to earn hers, not take them.

"Jimmy is the kindest man I've met, but he won't be buyin' ye gifts on an iceman's dime. All of ye turn around and shut yer eyes for a moment."

Bridie covered her eyes with her hands and Mary turned around to face the wall. Anna cleared her throat and looked at Helen.

"I'm closin' me eyes, don't ye fret." Helen placed her hands over her eyes, but she was keen on watching between her fingers.

Anna walked over to the wardrobe and opened a drawer above the linens. She pushed aside stockings and removed a cardboard box Helen had never seen before, then brought it over to the bed and took off its lid.

"I can assure ye we'll be throwin' the whole weddin' come October."

The sisters officially opened their eyes, but Helen knew they had all been peeking somehow.

Inside was more money than all of them made in a year combined.

CHAPTER 4

MARY'S ENGAGEMENT

—

"How do ye feel bein' the future Mrs. Jimmy Higgins?" Mary's new fiancé asked.

Mary stood facing Jimmy in front of her home's doorway. They had been engaged for an hour. The light from the window behind Jimmy cast a shadow over the left side of his round face, a first quarter moon. The oil in his hair had worn away with the day's mugginess, and the light illuminated the stray hairs sticking up every which way. His green eyes were black, shrunken irises and enlarged pupils melded together. He was more handsome than he'd ever been.

Taking his clammy hands in hers, she said, "It feels absolutely grand, like I've won a million dollars."

Jimmy cocked his head, the shadow moving to the right half of his face. "Not a million and one?"

Mary stepped forward to close the gap between them and wrapped her arms around his neck. "A million and two," she whispered.

"Do ye promise ye like the ring? I can take it back if ye—"

Mary leaned in and kissed Jimmy softly, then pulled back to enjoy his surprise at the kiss. "Me love, it's the most beautiful gift I've ever received."

He removed a hand from her waist and stroked her right cheek. "I've been savin' money since the day I passed ye in me truck outside St. Columba's after Sunday mornin' Mass let out. Ye were wearin' a green dress that reminded me of the rollin' hills of home, the tall, swayin' grass. I knew we'd be together forever if I mustered up the courage to introduce meself."

Mary searched his face like a map, trying to determine how she'd found treasure without even looking in the first place. Jimmy Higgins was the type of man sung about in songs. He loved his job delivering ice blocks to businesses. He always waved to the newsboys on the street corners of his route and threw pieces of his lunch to stray dogs running alongside his truck. Everyone in North Philadelphia called him "Whistlin' Jimmy." His propensity for pub tunes set him apart from every other delivery man in the city. She found it impossible not to love him.

Her vision blurred with tears of happiness. Her fingers and toes tingled as if she'd been out in frigid temperatures for too long. She choked back a cry. Jimmy had never seen her upset, but she couldn't fight the building emotion in her core. The tingling moved through her arms and legs like a growing ember until her whole body was on fire with a deeply unrealized joy. Mary threw herself forward and kissed her fiancé with more passion than she knew possible. Jimmy melted into the embrace and returned the intensity.

"The devil is turning more and more young people salacious these days," a shrill woman's voice said behind them, each word growing louder.

Breathing heavily, Mary untangled herself from Jimmy's clutch and avoided eye contact with the pair of conversing elderly ladies approaching them. She usually didn't care what others thought about her conduct, but something about being engaged made her suddenly self-conscious. She grabbed Jimmy's hand and pulled him onto the steps to let them pass. When they disappeared into the darkness, Mary closed her eyes and let out a sigh.

"Don't worry, we're not goin' to be arrested for public indecency." Jimmy laughed, rubbing her shoulders.

Mary folded her arms over her chest, aware of her disheveled appearance. "Another minute more, and I'm sure ye'd have me clothes off."

Jimmy looked up and down the street, then placed his hands on Mary's waist. "There's nothin' wrong with wantin' to see me future wife in all her beauty."

"Me sisters are probably listenin' behind the door!" Mary said, covering Jimmy's mouth with her hand.

He raised an eyebrow and nodded twice, so she lowered her hand. He had never been this forward with her about his desires. It took him nearly three weeks to kiss her on the cheek for the first time. Moving from her cheek to her lips was another frustrating two. Mary held his hand ten minutes into their first outing.

"There's just somethin' about puttin' a ring on ye that—"

"I don't know where ye're goin' with that thought, but I've got to get inside before I lose meself again."

"I think kissin' again might be—"

"Jimmy!"

He put his hands up in defeat and leaned in to peck her cheek. Mary hesitated but allowed it. Jimmy tucked a curl behind her ear and smiled.

"I love ye, Miss Mary Galvin. I really do."

Mary winked. "Ye and me both. Now run along home before me sisters open the door."

"Tell Bridie I hope she heals soon, and I'm excited to meet her."

"When she knows we're engaged, she's goin' to be hangin' on yer arm in no time."

"I have no trouble winnin' over all the Galvin girls."

"Oh hush. Go on now." Mary laughed, giving her fiancé a light push down the stairs.

Jimmy waved and turned left down the street, whistling a tune she knew but couldn't name. Mary watched him until the shadowy outline of his figure vanished into fading dusk. She looked down at her engagement ring. The round-cut diamond glittered under the window light as she moved her hand away from her body. She never wanted to take it off. She never dreamed a piece of jewelry could be this perfect.

A loud thud from inside snapped Mary out of her thoughts. It sounded like someone fell down the stairs. Was it Bridie? Could she have hit her head again? Was she unconscious? Blood everywhere? Mary tried turning the doorknob, but it was locked. She frantically opened her pocketbook and tried to find her house key, but it was too dark to see anything. She dropped the bag on the top step and crouched over it, pulling out hairpin after handkerchief until she found the key at the bottom. Not bothering to put the items back in the pocketbook, she stood up and jammed the key into the lock above the doorknob and fiddled until it clicked. Mary turned the knob and pushed open the door to see Helen, Anna, and Theresa standing on the staircase grinning at her.

"What happened? Who fell? Is Bridie well?" she asked, placing a hand over her racing heart.

Her sisters exchanged glances and laughed.

"Everythin' is positively fine. Theresa tripped and fell on her behind runnin' down the stairs when Helen spotted ye and Jimmy havin' a quite scandalous moment," Anna said, hopping off the bottom step to the floor.

"I almost fainted when I saw ye through the window upstairs. Bridie thought I saw the Lord returnin'," Helen added, her eyes wide.

Mary bit her lip and stared at the ground, heat collecting in her cheeks. Her sisters had never seen Jimmy kiss her, let alone run his hands through her hair and travel down to unmentionable areas. She tried to be a good girl, modest and honorable like their mother had raised them. Irish Catholic girls didn't dare have intimate relations before marriage. It was a grave and dirty sin. She and Jimmy hadn't technically done anything wrong.

From the middle of the staircase, Theresa pointed to Mary's left hand. "What's that? Is that what I think it is?"

She extended her hand to give her sisters a better view. "Jimmy and I are engaged!"

All three sisters gasped and pushed each other to get a closer glimpse. Anna took Mary's hand and examined the ring like the holy belonging of a famous saint. Helen and Theresa stood on either side of Anna and fawned over its beauty, looking from Mary's face to the ring multiple times.

"Jesus, Mary, and Joseph. How could Jimmy afford such a glamorous ring?" Helen asked, shaking her head.

Mary fanned herself with her right hand. "He said he's been savin' up since the day we met."

Theresa sighed quietly. "Oh, Mary, that's so romantic!"

"By the size, it must've cost him a hundred dollars," Anna said, raising her eyebrows.

Mary nodded. "He didn't tell me exactly, but the price doesn't matter to me. He could've spent five dollars, and I'd be the happiest girl in the world to call him me own."

"I wonder how long he's been holdin' onto it," Theresa said.

Helen looked at Mary. "It has to be at least a month. Remember when I saw him lookin' in the window of Smith's Jewelers in August? I wanted to follow him for a few days afterward, but Anna ruined me investigation."

Anna raised her chin and patted Helen on the back. "Because the Good Lord does not condone nosiness."

"Hello! What's goin' on down there?" Bridie called from upstairs.

Amid the excitement, Mary had forgotten Bridie was confined to her bed. With all the drama surrounding the locket earlier in the day, she hoped the ring would cheer her younger sister up. Mary closed the front door she'd left ajar in the panic and climbed the stairs, Anna, Helen, and Theresa following one by one. She peeked into the bedroom to avoid startling Bridie. She lay flat with two pillows propping up her bandaged head. With the blanket pulled up to her chin, she looked ready to fall asleep any moment. When Bridie realized Mary was there, she pushed the blanket down and waved her over to the bed.

"Did ye get engaged? Where's the ring?"

Mary sat down on the bed next to Bridie and held out her left hand. Bridie grabbed it and held it close to her face, her mouth agape.

"I've never seen anythin' so beautiful. May I try it on just for a moment?"

"Can't ye just be happy for yer sister?" Anna said as she walked in after Mary.

"I want to know what it feels like!"

Anna perched on the edge of the bed next to Mary. "Ye will know when ye're engaged to a fella someday, but hopefully that's far away because ye've got some growin' up to do."

Bridie huffed and continued to admire Mary's ring. "How did Jimmy ask ye to marry him?"

"Do ye really want to hear the story? It's not as excitin' as ye probably hope."

Helen and Theresa stepped away from the doorframe and took seats on the floor between the bed and the wall, folding their legs underneath their dresses. Bridie pushed herself into a higher seated position, and Anna turned her body fully to face Mary. She felt like a radio announcer ready to deliver breaking news with her sisters' undivided attention.

"Where do I start? Well, ye know I walked to the park alone to meet Jimmy."

Her sisters nodded eagerly.

"He didn't tell me exactly where to meet him, but we always meet by the duck pond at the west end. I believed he would be standin' there as usual."

"Was he there?" Bridie asked, clasping her hands together.

Anna scooted closer. "Was he already kneelin'?"

"He was there, but he wasn't kneelin'. He was sittin' on a nearby bench facin' the pond and—"

"Does he usually sit on the bench?"

Helen got to her knees and leaned against the bed. "Bridie, would ye please let Mary finish the story? I imagine all yer urgent questions will be answered in the next thought."

Bridie tilted her head to the left and rolled her eyes. Mary understood Helen's impatience, but they needed to remember Bridie was only sixteen, and she had been injured on her first day in America. She deserved understanding today no matter how many times she interrupted the story. In a month, though, Mary would certainly agree with Helen.

"I walked over to the bench where Jimmy was sittin' and squeezed his shoulder. He nearly jumped three feet in the air! I think he must've been rehearsin' the grand question in his thoughts. Well, after he realized it was me, he fell to his knees and started singin' 'When Irish Eyes Are Smilin'.'"

Her sisters glanced at each other and swooned, cupping their own cheeks.

"I stood there swayin' to his off-beat tune, just watchin' his eyes glitter. When he finished, I asked him why he sang that song, and he was quiet a moment. His lip quiverin', he reached into his jacket pocket and pulled out the ring. He said I was his Ireland, his beautiful home."

"Ye're not lyin'? He actually said such a thing?" Helen asked, placing her elbows on the edge of the bed.

Anna pointed to the pressed rose laying on the bedside table. "Of course, he did! He's the same Jimmy Higgins who showed up with five bouquets of roses on Mary's birthday because he didn't know which color she'd fancy."

Mary didn't realize she'd been smiling since she sat down. The corners of her mouth shook like Father Lange's arms after holding up the altar bread for too long. But she didn't care. She hadn't smiled this much since Jimmy brought her to a Sunday neighborhood dance in June and spun her for hours.

"He didn't even ask me to marry him. I just said yes."

"I'm not surprised in the least. Ye're always puttin' words in his mouth," Anna said.

Helen sat back on her heels. "Jesus, Mary, and Joseph, we have so much plannin' to do. There's the dress, the invitations, the food, the church, the honeymoon, the date—"

"Ye don't need to fret about the date. We're gettin' married on October 2. Jimmy wants to honor his grandparents' anniversary since their passin'."

Her sisters gasped in unison. Helen stood up and hurried over to the wardrobe. She opened the top drawer and fetched the *Farmers' Almanac*. Leafing through the pages, she walked back to the bed and sat on the floor.

"Oh, Mary, ye can't get married on October 2. It's a Wednesday! That's the middle of the workin' week," Helen said, turning the book around to show her.

"Mother says it's bad luck if ye don't get married on a Sunday," Bridie added.

Mary stopped smiling for the first time all evening. "Hush, all of ye. A Wednesday will do just fine. It's important to Jimmy, and I want to respect his wishes. The date is settled, and I will figure everythin' else out. The next step is plannin' where to get married."

"Ye're not gettin' married at St. Columba's?" Anna and Helen said at the same time.

"That's what I intend, but when I mentioned it to Jimmy, he said he needed to speak with a few people before makin' a decision."

Anna clicked her tongue. "A devout Catholic man wouldn't need to speak with anyone but the Lord."

CHAPTER 5

BRIDIE'S FIRST DAY AT O'HARA'S

Bridie had been standing across the street from O'Hara's Beauty Parlor for ten minutes, watching women come in and out like a confessional before Sunday morning Mass. She was supposed to meet Helen's friend, Mira Jameson, at eleven o'clock, but she caught her reflection in a parked car's window just before reaching the building. The bandage on her forehead was hideous. She looked like a wounded soldier straight from the trenches. It had been a week since the incident, and Dr. Burns assured her the gash was healing quite well. The extended purple bruising below her eyebrow and under her eye suggested otherwise. Never mind the bleeding had stopped and the stitches had been removed. The right half of her face was ghastly, and the concerned stares from passersby on the walk there confirmed it. And Anna's red lipstick she borrowed most definitely clashed with her hair color.

Going home wasn't a possibility. It was Helen's usual day off and she ran errands all morning and afternoon, returning to the house at unplanned times. Bridie could explore the city for a few hours, but then she'd receive unwelcome stares. The last thing she wanted to do was draw more attention to herself. St. Columba's wasn't too far of a walk, and she remembered Anna saying the main hall was usually empty until choir rehearsal in the evenings. Taking a nap on a wooden pew in a dimly lit church didn't seem like such a terrible idea. The Lord took pity on the blind and deaf, so why not the ugly?

On second thought, the Lord rewarded hard work and sacrifice. Meeting with Mira Jameson in front of all the beautiful, rich women of upper-class Philadelphia would unarguably be a sacrifice of dignity. And standing for hours watching Mira style hair would certainly be hard work. Her legs would grow achy and splotchy, matching the discoloration of her face—a true public sacrifice.

She pulled out Mary's powder compact from her borrowed pocketbook. She had sneaked the compact from the basket on Mary's side of the bed she shared with Anna. Dr. Burns told her putting any makeup near the wound would infect it, so all her sisters hid their makeup, aside from lipstick. Luckily, Bridie learned Mary was a terrible liar the moment she found her older sister halfway under the bed hiding her makeup. Her excuse was she spotted a mouse and wanted to catch it before Anna saw it and fainted. She knew Anna wasn't afraid of mice. When Bridie was eight, she had rescued and kept a field mouse as a pet. Anna almost wanted it for herself.

Glaring at herself in the compact's mirror, Bridie dabbed a near-white powder around her eye to lighten the bruising. It now seemed as if she hadn't slept at all, but she preferred that to looking like a donkey kicked her in the face. The tape holding the bandage to her forehead was peeling back, so she pressed it down, squinting in discomfort. If the bandage fell off in O'Hara's, she'd never be able to show her face again. Back in Listowel, gossip spread through town like pneumonia in January, and it was probably worse in American high society. The last thing she needed was to be blacklisted from every beauty shop in the city and forced to work in a windowless factory for eight hours a day doing the same task. She swore to be different from her sisters.

Bridie inhaled deeply and closed the compact, then placed it back in her pocketbook. Everything would be fine. She waited for oncoming traffic to pass before crossing the street. A light breeze brushed her curls in front of her eyes as she stepped onto the sidewalk. Not seeing the slight difference in height, she tripped over the curb and fell onto her hands and knees. Bridie glanced around to check if anyone had seen the ungraceful stumble. No one but the Lord. Relieved, she stood up and peered down at her floral dress. It was still pressed to perfection, but her stockings were ripped at both knees. A couple scratches, but no blood.

"Are you Helen's sister?"

Bridie looked up to see a young woman approaching her from O'Hara's. She wore a white, embroidered apron over her blouse and skirt. A pair of scissors peeked out from one of the pockets. The sun reflected off her blonde finger waves, making the hue practically match her apron.

"Yes, I'm Bridie. Are ye Miss Jameson?"

"Please call me Mira," she said, extending a hand.

Bridie went to return the gesture but realized the base of her palm was bleeding from the fall. She retracted her hand and hid it behind her back.

Mira lowered her hand to her side. "Are you seriously hurt? I saw you trip when I peeked out the door to see if you were coming."

"No, I'm just fine. Only a bit scratched up around the knees," Bridie said, her voice trailing off at the end. She was surprised Mira didn't immediately jump to her obvious forehead bandage.

"We can get you cleaned up in the back before you start training." Mira pointed toward the salon.

"Oh yes, I don't want to be near any clients lookin' like a complete travesty."

"Darling, you look absolutely radiant for a girl who was practically robbed!"

Bridie snorted. "I suppose Helen told ye about the incident last week."

Mira placed a hand on Bridie's shoulder and lowered her chin. "To start a new job a week after hitting your head on the sidewalk deserves an entire column in the society page. You should be the talk of the town."

"I certainly will be with this bandage on me—"

"Bandage? It's a badge for your courage!" Mira said, linking arms with Bridie. They walked together, steps in sync, to the salon entrance.

When Bridie stepped inside, she didn't know where to look. Every part of the beauty shop had movement and noise. Four women sat in the waiting area by the door, two of them chatting while the others paged through clothing catalogs. Each of the eight leather chairs held a client engrossed in conversation with her stylist—gesturing, pointing, nodding. Wisps of hair fell to the floor with every snip of blades. The furnace whistled above the blowing hair dryers. Bridie's eyes rested on the farthest corner where an older woman sat under a large machine that attached what looked like curlers to her hair. Two dozen must have been extended from above, like a mad scientist's experiment.

Mira turned to Bridie and giggled. "I'm guessing you've never seen a permanent wave machine before."

She shook her head. The salon in Listowel was nowhere near as busy and didn't have any machines due to lack of electricity. Women only went to the beauty parlor if a special occasion arose, like a family wedding. Otherwise, they styled their own hair. Her mother plaited her hair every day until Grady O'Leary cut it off. For a while after, it was only long enough to sleep in rag curls.

"It works really well unless you move around too much and burn your scalp."

Bridie's eyes widened. She'd definitely be sticking to rag curls for the time being.

"Mira, who's the new girl?" another stylist asked as she walked by with a handful of hairpins.

"Samantha, this is Bridie Galvin. She starts training as my assistant today."

The pear-shaped woman stopped in front of Bridie and looked her up and down with distaste.

"What happened to you? Fall off the back of a paddy wagon?"

Bridie stared down at her shoes. Of course, the leather on the right toe was scuffed.

"Samantha, don't be rude now," Mira said, placing a hand on her hip. "Bridie has been through quite enough in the last week and doesn't need your judgment. Your own curls are somewhat out of place. I'd go take a look in a mirror. You don't want your next client to doubt your skills."

"Hmph." Samantha turned sharply around and headed toward the back of the salon.

Mira lifted Bridie's chin with one finger. "Don't mind her, darling. Her fiancé broke off their engagement last week, and she's still sulking over a future that was never going to happen. Trust me."

"Me sister Mary actually just got engaged."

"You don't say! Who's the lucky fella?" Mira asked, clapping her hands.

"Jimmy Higgins. I haven't met him yet, but he's supposed to be comin' round for dinner on Friday."

"Oh, he's such a sweetheart. I've run into him a few times at the dances. How long had they been goin' steady?"

"I think a year and some. Enough that it's not scandalous for me mother."

"Scandalous? Over a year is downright taking their precious time." Mira lowered her voice to a whisper. "Samantha and her fella had only been courting for three weeks. Can you even imagine? I heard he was with another woman."

Bridie covered her mouth to laugh. She felt a little giddy knowing the salon gossip already and completely understood why Helen and Mira got along so well. They met at last year's Mummers Parade on New Year's Day, whatever that was. Helen had tried to explain it to her, but she gave up when Bridie asked if the Mummers marched the whole route mum. They both loved being on the inside and having important information about others at their fingertips. Helen assured Bridie she never gossiped salaciously; that was a dreadful sin.

Mira looked at the clock above the door. "Goodness, I didn't realize it was a quarter to noon already! It's time for your first lesson."

She strolled over to the waiting area on their right and stopped in front of a plump middle-aged woman reading *Good Housekeeping*. "Mrs. Nichols, are you ready for your appointment?"

The woman looked up and smiled widely enough to reveal two missing teeth. "Good morning, Mira. I am more than ready to fix the rat's nest on my head."

Mira led Mrs. Nichols over to an empty chair in front of a pristine mirror. Bridie hesitated to follow because she hadn't cleaned up as planned. Her palms were still caked in dried blood. She didn't want to put off the client by her indecent appearance. Mira caught Bridie's attention and waved her over.

"Mrs. Nichols, I'd like you to meet my new assistant, Bridie Galvin."

Their client turned around in her chair and gasped, then looked at Mira with disgust, her upper lipped curled. "Why does she look like that? Did she get hit by a trolley?"

"No, ma'am. She was almost robbed last week and took a hard fall. Isn't that right, Bridie?"

Mira and Mrs. Nichols both looked at her. She didn't know whether to speak or just nod silently like when addressing a nun.

Mrs. Nichols narrowed her eyes. "Are you slow, girl?"

Bridie bit her lip and shook her head. "No, ma'am."

"Good. If you intend on styling my hair, I expect you to learn quickly. Mira is an expert."

Mira gave Bridie a tight-lipped smile and spun Mrs. Nichols back around toward the mirror.

"Alright, Mrs. Nichols. What's the occasion for today's style?" Mira asked, placing a black cape around her client's shoulders.

"My husband is hosting potential new business colleagues for dinner, and they recently won big on the stock market when it peaked last week. I have to look absolutely divine to impress their wives enough to give a good word about my husband. He wants to buy shares in their company."

"We will make you much greater than divine. You will look simply exquisite."

Mira removed Mrs. Nichols's hat and gave it to Bridie to hold while watching. She retrieved a comb from her apron pocket and brushed out the curls one at a time, removing hairpins when necessary.

"The stock market is really doing well these days, but there's talk of a dip coming soon," Mrs. Nichols said, looking at her nails. "My husband said some are worried about the economic bubble bursting."

"I don't really follow the market, as I've never invested," Mira said, turning her head to look at Bridie. "Have you?"

She hesitated to speak. "I'm afraid I know nothin'…but me sister Anna got lucky recently and surprised us."

Mrs. Nichols nodded, making eye contact with Bridie in the mirror. "Your sister is smart. Buying shares, even a couple, as a working woman can go far. What does she plan on doing with the money?"

"Me other sister Mary is gettin' married in about a month, so it'll help pay for the weddin'. I think the rest will go into the bank."

"The late spring is better for a wedding, but I suppose October will do if it doesn't rain."

A short brunette stylist with bangs walked up behind Mira and tapped her shoulder. "I'm sorry to interrupt, but you have an urgent phone call from your mother."

Mira opened her mouth to protest, but Mrs. Nichols waved her off. "Combing out curls isn't difficult. It'll test Bridie's skills with little training. A simpleton could do it right."

Bridie's face felt hot like a sudden fever spike. "Oh, I don't know if I—"

"It will only take a few moments, darling. I'll be right back," Mira said, squeezing Bridie's upper arm and handing her the comb.

"Are you going to start? I don't want to be here all day."

Bridie placed Mrs. Nichols's hat on the nearest counter and rubbed her hands on her dress, hoping most of the dried blood flaked off. She didn't need it falling into her client's scalp like rust-colored dandruff. Stepping close behind the chair, she replicated Mira's soft but swift motions of combing each curl.

"My husband has a new secretary, Miss Rodney. He's been spending extra time in the office later in the evening and going in early on other days. My friends are convinced he's having an affair with her."

Bridie averted her eyes from Mrs. Nichols' gaze in the mirror. The last time she engaged in a conversation about an affair, she was twelve years old and being accused of seducing away her best friend's fella with a fresh scone. She didn't know anything about real relationships or marriage.

"I suppose you're normally a pretty young thing. How do I lure my husband away from her?"

"I'm sorry to interrupt, but I wanted to let you both know that I must catch a trolley home," Mira said with an enormous grin. "My sister has gone into labor with her first child, and I'm to be the godmother!"

"That's absolutely wonderful, Mira! Yes, do run along before the child arrives," Mrs. Nichols said, waving her off.

Mira turned to Bridie. "I will get another stylist to take over the appointment. You can train with her for the rest of the afternoon, and I should be back on Thursday."

"That won't be necessary, Mira. Bridie is doing fine, and we're enjoying an enthralling conversation. She was just about to give me some much-needed advice."

"I wouldn't doubt it for a moment. Her sister Helen spoke so highly of her styling skills."

Mrs. Nichols nodded. "Of course, now go and see about your sister!"

Mira grabbed her shawl from the back of the salon and ran out the door, leaving Bridie to Mrs. Nichols once again.

"Where were we? Oh yes, what shall I do about my husband's potential affair?"

Bridie hesitated. She didn't want to insult or embarrass her first client, or she could be out of a job before Mira returned. At the same time, she needed to give valid advice or Mrs. Nichols would probably think she was incompetent, or even worse, she could completely ruin an established marriage. The Holy Ghost needed to take hold of her tongue.

"Did you hear me?"

"Mrs. Nichols, I think ye should speak with Samantha, another stylist. I've heard she's had a similar experience and could probably offer better advice. Just don't tell her ye heard it from me."

CHAPTER 6

THERESA'S SECOND JOB

———

The raw blisters on Theresa's heels burned like hot coals with her every step. Borrowing Helen's extra pair of work shoes had been a terrible idea. The soles on her own shoes had worn through completely, and the cobbler said he wouldn't have them ready until Thursday. That left her with two options: Mary's extra-large shoes or Helen's child-sized ones. Anna's feet were practically the same size, but she only had one pair. For fairly old shoes worn every day, they were in pristine condition, much like everything else Anna owned.

Theresa had already walked two miles from the factory in Helen's tight shoes, her toes scrunched and squeezed. She still had another mile left before meeting Bridie outside O'Hara's and walking yet another mile home together. Anna and Mary were supposed to pick Bridie up with her, but they needed to stop by the grocer's to pick up ingredients for Friday's much-anticipated dinner with Jimmy Higgins, their soon-to-be brother-in-law. This family dinner would be the first of many before the early October celebration. She intended to make their mother's brown bread with raisins. If Jimmy didn't like the bread, he'd never fit into the family. Mother's rule.

She hoped Anna and Mary would meet her in time at O'Hara's. It was Bridie's first day there, and really, her first day in public. Bridie had refused to leave the house for an entire week, even though Dr. Burns said the fresh air would do her some good. Theresa understood the discomfort Bridie felt, but she never shared the same preoccupation with appearance despite only being a year apart. Curled hair and a small nose didn't make a strong woman. When Helen told Bridie she'd have to meet Mira Jameson this morning or lose the opportunity, Bridie agreed without much fuss. She only stood in front of the mirror for a half hour—a new record for the week. The new job would force her to focus more on others' vanity and less on her own.

Theresa kept walking. She winced with the physical pain and the realization of what Bridie may have experienced today. Upper-class women could be terribly judgmental. While Theresa didn't care about the hen chatter now, her first experience as the target of whispers was mortifying. She wore an outdated hat to a parish picnic, and by the end of it, she threw the hat out. Wide-brimmed sun hats were only for fieldworkers who hoed potatoes out of the ground. If they criticized her handmade hat that much in her presence, Theresa couldn't imagine what they possibly said to Bridie about her bandage and bruising. To be honest, she didn't know if Bridie could endure the harshness. She had always been temperamental.

Her walk slowed to a trudge as she passed by the same park where Jimmy had proposed to Mary. Young mothers sat on blankets while their children danced and played around them, pointing at the sky. A number also pushed baby carriages along the paved path around a large pond. They mouthed lullabies and stopped every few steps to push their carriage back and forth in place. She didn't see a single man, not that she was surprised. The men worked and the women stayed home. It was expected.

Just as she turned her gaze away from the park, a leather ball hit her right ankle. She picked it up and searched for its owner. A grinning boy, maybe five or six years old, peeked out from behind a tree to her left. He pointed to the ball in her hands. Theresa waved at him, smiling. He skipped over and jumped in front of her with two feet.

"Is this yer ball?" she asked, holding it out.

He nodded and took it, cradling it like a newborn.

"What's yer name?"

The boy looked down at the ground. "Michael."

"Ye have such a handsome name, like the great St. Michael."

He looked up at Theresa through his long lashes.

"Is yer mother somewhere in the park?" Theresa pointed behind him.

Michael nodded again, holding the ball tighter.

Theresa crouched down to his height. "Will ye bring me to her? I'll follow ye. Ye'll be the leader."

He flashed his missing front teeth, then spun around and ran straight between the trees that bordered the park.

"Michael, slow down! I can't run as fast as ye," she called after him.

The boy didn't slow down until he reached a mother sitting on a blanket with an infant in each arm. Theresa caught up a moment later, her heels practically numb after running the short distance. Slightly out of breath, she walked to Michael's mother with her hands on her hips.

"I'm sorry to bother ye...but I wanted to make sure...yer son returned safely," she said, still catching her breath.

"You're not a bother in the least! Thank you for bringing him back," the mother said, bouncing her babies.

She was absolutely radiant sitting in the sun with her legs folded under her light blue dress. Her cheeks were perfectly rosy amid a backdrop of freckles. She had not a brown hair out of place, even with a noticeable wind. In a more formal gown and men on her arms instead of two babies, she would be mistaken for a Hollywood star.

"It's me pleasure. I used to look out for me younger siblings all the time back home."

"Sometimes I want to rip my hair out when Michael goes running off. I have four-month-old twins and can't chase after him like I used to before they were born."

"Oh yes, I completely understand. Me mother had twelve children, so she had the older children watch the younger ones while she took care of the babies."

The woman's eyes widened. "Twelve children! I can barely take care of three on my own while my husband works over-time at Apex Hosiery."

Theresa laughed. "Me mother used to pray the Rosary at least twice a day to give her patience and grace."

"I suppose the number of children doesn't matter. Motherhood is not easy."

"May I hold one of yer babies?" Theresa asked, kneeling down onto the blanket.

"Yes please! My arm was just starting to tingle."

Theresa moved closer and leaned in to transfer the baby from the mother's arms to hers.

"You're holding Margaret, but we call her Maggie."

Theresa looked down at the baby girl in her arms. From the green jumper, she couldn't tell the gender initially, but the large blue eyes gave her away. Those eyes would indeed break many hearts. Holding Maggie felt so natural, as if she were Theresa's own child.

"She's absolutely beautiful. What's her twin's name?"

"George. A boy and a girl to satisfy both myself and my husband." She laughed. Her high trills sounded like a wind chime.

"The Lord blessed ye well. I wish to have many children someday, but I have to meet the right man first!"

"I suspect you're young, but don't worry yourself one bit. You'll meet him in time. I didn't meet my husband until I was twenty."

Maggie fussed, so Theresa rocked and hushed her. She calmed down almost immediately.

"I've never been able to quiet her that quickly. You're going to be a natural mother," the woman said, shaking her head in disbelief.

"Thank ye...oh, I never got yer name!"

"My goodness, of course. I'm Penny Grant. And you are?"

Theresa froze. Penny Grant. She recognized the last name. Anna's new supervisor was Harry Grant. He was supposedly the kindest and youngest supervisor in the factory. Many workers on her floor gushed about him, but Anna disliked him. She never revealed why but warned against being alone with him. He was supposedly quite handsome, but Theresa had never seen him since she worked on a different floor. The rumor was his wife had recently given birth to twins.

"Mrs. Grant, it's a pleasure to meet ye. Ye can call me Theresa."

"Please call me Penny. Mrs. Grant is my mother-in-law."

"Very well, Penny. I apologize, but I must get goin' to meet me sister at O'Hara's."

"Before you go, may I ask you something?"

"Of course!" Theresa shifted Maggie to her other arm, careful not to wake her.

Penny cleared her throat. "I know we just met, but I've been looking for some extra help with the children. My husband returns home so late sometimes, and I admit I have trouble handling both the children and the household chores. We moved here from Connecticut just before I gave birth, so I have no family to give me a hand when I need to cook and put the children to bed."

Theresa hesitated. This would be the perfect opportunity to be around children without stopping every mother to coo at her baby on the walk to and from the factory. She'd also make some extra money for the holidays coming up, since Mary's wedding would be expensive. At the same time, Penny's husband was Anna's boss, the very one she explicitly was told to stay away from. But she wouldn't ever be alone with Harry Grant. And she'd been helping Mrs. McCormick in the evenings lately with her ill mother, so taking the job wouldn't be too risky. Anna just couldn't find out.

"I would be honored to help ye, Penny, even if it's only for a night or two a week."

Penny squealed with excitement. "Michael, come over here!"

The boy kicked his ball over to the blanket and stared at his mother.

"Would you like Theresa to come over and play with you before bed?"

Michael smiled at the ground, picked up his ball, and ran back to where he was playing.

"That's his way of saying he's ecstatic," Penny said, bouncing George again. "I suppose it's settled then. I can give you a call tomorrow to talk about the details. What's your full name? I want to make sure I'm reaching the right household by telephone."

"Oh, it's Theresa…Dwyer." She couldn't take a chance of word traveling back to Anna about her taking the job. "But there's no need to call me. I can just come by yer home on Thursday evenin'. I know ye're mighty busy with the children and other duties."

"You're right, I can hardly stay on a telephone call for more than thirty seconds without one of the babies crying. Why don't you arrive by eight o'clock on Thursday evening? I live at 1617 Fairmount Avenue, which isn't too far of a walk I hope."

"No, not at all. I will be there right on time. Would ye like me to bring anythin'?"

Penny thought a moment, looking down at George. "I don't think so. I should let you go meet your sister now. I've kept you much too long."

Theresa smiled and leaned in to transfer Maggie back to her mother. The baby awoke and started whimpering.

"Looks like I already need you," Penny said, bouncing the babies in sync.

"I promise I'll be back on Thursday at eight o'clock sharp." Theresa stood up from the blanket and brushed some grass from her dress. She waved to Michael in the distance when she caught his eye. He raised his ball and slammed it to the ground.

Theresa chuckled and started in the direction of the street.

"I almost forgot!" Penny called after her.

Theresa turned around.

"My husband doesn't know about my bringing in extra help, so don't tell anyone."

Or she'd most certainly be out of both jobs.

CHAPTER 7

ANNA'S INVESTIGATION

The end of the workweek sneaked up on Anna. The monotonous eight-hour shifts ran together like the forty days of Lent every spring, Fridays marking the passage of time with potato soup. The Lord forbade eating meat. Thank goodness it wasn't Lent, though. It was September, and she intended on impressing Jimmy Higgins with a hearty pot roast for the evening's celebratory engagement dinner. Mary rarely brought Jimmy home for fear of embarrassment, but when she did, his visits were brief. After more than a year of going steady, the sisters knew only Jimmy well through Mary's anecdotes. Today was Anna's chance. Bridie wasn't working at the salon today, so Anna instructed her to go to the butcher's to pick up the beef cutlet in the afternoon. It'd still be fresh by the time she arrived home. Not as fresh as on the farm, but it would do.

Anna walked on the shady side of the street. Early autumn was much sunnier than she was used to. Once the first of September came to Listowel, it rained at least once a day until the first of June the following year. She never had to worry about freckles appearing or her skin turning pink. Rouge took care of that matter. The American sun branded her as a true farmer's daughter, no matter how much she resented it.

She slowed her pace upon approaching the grand entrance to John Wanamaker's. The floor-to-ceiling windows gave much more than a glimpse into a shopping spree wonderland. The city's most lavish department store had every product thinkable crowding its multiple floors, or so Anna imagined. She had never dared to take one step inside. The wealthy women donning diamond jewelry sets and spotless silk gloves were enough to keep her admiring from afar. She watched them carelessly sashay from one counter to another in the Grand Court, trying on pearls and sampling lipsticks. They waved employees away when fancying themselves in hand mirrors.

Cupping her hands against the window, Anna almost pressed her nose to the glass. On the far end of the marble-clad atrium was the largest pipe organ she'd ever seen. The countless golden pipes glimmered as the sunlight shone through the cathedral-esque windows. Famous organists gave holiday concerts to those who could afford tickets, but the angelic music could be heard for blocks. Just below the organ sat the impressive bronze eagle statue that greeted entering shoppers. An acquaintance at St. Columba's once told her both the organ and eagle statue had appeared at the 1904 World's Fair in St. Louis. The centuries-old ruins of Listowel Castle she grew up revering felt insignificant in comparison. With its multistory stone archway and slit windows for shooting arrows, the castle loomed over the town square. After running errands for her mother, Anna often sat in the castle's shadow and imagined the battles that ensued inside the walls.

Like the castle, she could stand in front of Wanamaker's and watch for hours. The department store was a snow globe that didn't need to be shaken. Flecks of dust came alive in the same sunbeams that lit up the pipe organ. She was an outsider, but those preserved inside couldn't see the swirling magic in the right light. This was their everyday. Buying five custom-made dresses in their world was like purchasing five bruised apples for her. And even though she'd won a year's salary playing the stock market, she refused to spend it on anything for herself. It wasn't only her money. Helen and Mary didn't know she used some of their own salaries to buy shares. Not the majority, but enough to feel guilty about taking it. She thanked the Lord three times every day for keeping the market up.

Anna took one last gaze at the world she wished to join, then turned away. She needed to get home to start the roast. That was her duty to Mary. Jimmy had never tasted their cooking, but he was convinced Mary could cook. Mary burned everything she put in the oven, so Anna volunteered to make the roast and tell Jimmy that Mary had made it. She believed a good wife must be a good cook, no matter how many jobs she worked outside the home. Jimmy obviously loved Mary. If she learned at least to cook their mother's cottage pie and beef stew between now and the wedding, Jimmy could only love her more. Their mother had tried to teach them all to cook, but Mary never took to it like her sisters. She enjoyed tasting the food more.

Shuffling toward the entrance, Anna observed the exiting shoppers. They were all the same. Pairs of women dressed in the finest couture only to be worn once, holding stunning handbags that would cost six months' rent. Not a single one held the door for the woman behind her. It was a parade of slamming doors and clicking heels and gossiping voices.

Until Jimmy Higgins strolled out.

Anna spun around and pulled down her hat. What was he doing at Wanamaker's? Why wasn't he wearing his uniform? His deliveries lasted until at least five o'clock because his truck always passed on her walk home. Anna had finished her duties earlier than usual and had left an hour early. It was only half past four. Had he finished his rounds early, too? What did he need to purchase? How could he afford to buy whatever it was? She peeked over her shoulder. Jimmy was headed in the other direction, the way home. She needed to go the same way, so she wouldn't technically be following him out of curiosity. She wasn't stalking him like Helen had attempted. She needed to put the roast in the oven for Mary. Simple.

The sidewalk was crowded enough to stay hidden without seeming suspicious. Jimmy walked about two motorcar lengths ahead, a tan package tucked under his left arm. His right arm swung to the rhythm of his faint whistling. He tipped his hat at every person who passed. A few delivery trucks honked from the road. His pace quickened as they neared the next cross street. Anna needed to close the distance between them, so she stepped around the group of men smoking cigarettes in front of her. Jimmy turned the corner and disappeared. If she followed him, she wouldn't be going home anymore.

Why did she need to go after him? He'd never done anything to upset Mary. He could've been picking up a package from Wanamaker's for someone else. Maybe he delivered ice to the restaurant upstairs and they called him in for another order. Perhaps he needed to make the last payment on the engagement ring if he bought it there. There were so many possibilities. If he caught her following him, she could claim it was all a coincidence and strike up a conversation. Then, they would have something to talk about at dinner. The pot roast could wait a half hour or so.

Anna hurried toward the cross street but stopped right before the edge of the building. She backed up against the brick wall and peered around the corner. Jimmy stood only a few feet away. He was in line to get on the same trolley she sometimes took home when she was too exhausted to walk. How would she get on without drawing attention to herself? Anna watched people climb onto the trolley one by one. When Jimmy got on, she took a deep breath, counted to three, and walked around the building to join the back of the line. She kept her gaze on the ground, only looking up with her eyes under the brim of her cloche.

With five people ahead of her in line, the trolley would be almost full by the time she reached the front. Every window had at least one face visible. She couldn't see Jimmy from where she stood. He was probably in the back. Anna took two steps forward. A seat in the first row would do. He wouldn't recognize the back of her head. Another two steps. She could see which stop he got off at without being noticed. And she'd still be going home. One more step. What if they got off at the same stop? What if he was going to see Mary?

"Ma'am, I can't let you get on without paying."

Anna looked up from the ground to the conductor staring at her. He pointed toward the payment box.

"I'm sorry, sir. I wasn't payin' attention," she said, reaching into her pocketbook to grab a coin. She dropped it into the box and nodded as she took the first open seat, keeping her head down.

She didn't look up to see where Jimmy sat, but the volume of his whistling was fairly low. He must've found a seat toward the back. The conductor shut the door and the trolley jerked forward. Passengers chatted behind her, but she couldn't make out any conversations with the loud clacking of the wheels. The trolley turned left onto the street where she and Jimmy had been walking. Automobiles drove alongside the trolley, many of them coated in a pale-yellow pollen. It hadn't rained in almost a week, and the ragweed around the city was blooming more each day.

Hopefully, Bridie picked up some flowers from the stand outside the butcher's after getting the meat. Anna hated having guests over for a proper dinner without a vase of fresh flowers on the table. A seasonable centerpiece always ensured a point of discussion if the conversation ever lulled. Although if Jimmy was as much a gentleman as they believed, he would show up with flowers. Or was the package from Wanamaker's a housewarming gift? Anna smiled to herself and shifted in her seat. The ladies at St. Columba's would be terribly jealous with her new crystal vase or set of embroidered linen serviettes.

The trolley was only a few streets from the stop closest to her house, and Jimmy still hadn't gotten off. If he was coming to see Mary before dinner, Anna knew she wouldn't be there. Mary always went to Confession on Fridays in the late afternoon. Why didn't he know that? Helen and Theresa wouldn't be home either because they clocked out at five and walked back at a goose's pace. Bridie may have already arrived from the butcher's, but she wouldn't answer the door if Jimmy knocked. Bridie wanted to impress him with the dress Mary gave her in exchange for her silence. She promised not to tell any humiliating stories. And it would take at least an hour for Bridie to get ready.

If she and Jimmy got off together, it would be impolite not to invite him inside. But she needed to start the pot roast. How could she prepare supper with her guest sitting in the dining room? What if he asked about her getting on the same trolley? Anna never lied. Helen would smack her across the face for revealing she followed him. Mary would run out of the room and cry in shame. Theresa and Bridie would snicker in the corner like the callow girls they were. Anna felt light-headed. She bowed her head and shut her eyes.

She opened her eyes as the trolley slowed down. It didn't normally stop on this part of the street.

"Thank ye for stoppin', sir!" Jimmy called, coming up the aisle.

Anna gasped and turned her head toward the window. Jimmy stepped off the trolley and walked in front of it to cross the street. The conductor shut the door and the trolley moved forward once again. She kept her eyes on him as he jogged up the sidewalk past a number of businesses and homes. Her heart beat faster as he approached the one place no Irish Catholic ever went inside. The trolley sped up, so Anna twisted to watch Jimmy growing smaller behind her.

He opened the door to St. John's Church and entered with a wide grin. Anna gasped and clutched her purse. He couldn't be...What business could he possibly have there? Was it true? Did Mary know? Was the Lord trying to punish them? Anna shut her eyes and let out a slow breath.

Jimmy Higgins was a Protestant.

CHAPTER 8

JIMMY HIGGINS COMES TO DINNER

When Jimmy knocked at the front door, Anna nearly dropped the pot roast. It was exactly seven o'clock. The mashed potatoes and green beans were already on the dining room table, steam escaping from underneath the dish lids. Helen had just finished slicing their mother's traditional brown bread and arranging the pieces artfully in a wicker basket lined with a red linen serviette. Theresa had polished the silverware spotless and inspected the china for chips before laying them out properly at every place setting. Helen had bought it secondhand at the parish swap sale for a bargain. The candles on either side of the floral centerpiece just needed to be lit. Everything was ready, but Anna wasn't.

"Helen and Theresa, can ye finish up what ye're doin' and start carvin'?" Anna asked, sliding the pot roast tray onto the stove. "Mary's still dressin' Bridie upstairs, so I'll answer the door."

"She's not meetin' Pope Pius," Helen said, walking into the dining room with the breadbasket.

Theresa shrugged and opened a drawer. "Maybe she has it in her mind that he's got younger brothers."

"Don't ye go givin' her any ideas now!" Anna struck Theresa's back end with a wound dishrag.

Theresa spun around with a newly sharpened knife, two hands on the wooden handle and a mischievous grin on her face. Anna pointed to the roast and walked to the front door without batting an eye. She needed to stay focused on her primary task—keeping Jimmy's horrid secret for the entire evening.

Mary had returned from Confession only a half hour ago while Anna was running around the kitchen. Bridie had called Mary to her bedroom as soon as she stepped in the door, so Anna didn't have a chance to speak with her. The others couldn't know before Mary, especially not Helen. She'd pull him by the ear all the way to St. Columba's for a quick Catholic conversion, if such a thing existed.

Protestants usually hailed from Northern Ireland, which remained part of the United Kingdom after the Irish War of Independence in 1921, but Jimmy had said his family was rooted in County Mayo. If any Protestants were from Mayo, they were run out by the Catholics for being traitorous British sympathizers. Jimmy was much kinder than the demons their mother made Protestants out to be. Almost Catholic. That's what a Protestant hiding his sin would want her to think.

A second knock sounded. Anna held her breath and opened the door. Jimmy stepped back and extended a bouquet of yellow daisies with a white ribbon tied around the stems.

"Good evenin', Miss Anna! These are for yer lovely table. Daisies are me mother's favorite," he said, taking off his hat with his free hand.

Anna took the flowers and smiled. "That's sweet, Jimmy. Thank ye."

She pulled back the front door further and gestured for him to enter. Shuffling past her, Jimmy smelled strongly of incense and cigarettes. Did he share a couple laughs and smokes with the Protestant pastor before coming? Anna relaxed her shoulders as she shut and locked the door. She laid the flowers gently on the entryway table.

"Where's me beautiful Mary?" Jimmy asked, looking up the staircase.

"She's helpin' Bridie get all pretty for ye, but she'll be down in a moment. Why don't ye have a seat at the table?"

Anna guided Jimmy down the hallway with a hand on his upper back. The dinner needed to be over by eight o'clock for her own sanity. When they reached the dining room, she pulled out the chair at the head of the table. She usually sat there, but for once she didn't want everyone's gaze on her. Bridie's new habit of repeating every piece of gossip from the beauty shop should keep everyone entertained.

Jimmy took the head seat and glanced around the room. He had never been past the foyer. Their dining room was nothing fancy, but it was presentable. A rectangular oak table large enough to squeeze eight chairs took up most of the space, except for a matching hutch against the wall opposite the entrance to the kitchen. The remaining red-papered walls were covered in ornaments the sisters had collected over the years. A few decorative porcelain plates in a diagonal. St. Brigid's cross made from woven rushes, now splintering. A painting of their parents Theresa had done from memory. Two hand mirrors, one turned inward to display the decorative backside and the other turned outward to reflect the joy in the room.

"He's much more handsome than ye described," Bridie said, following Mary into the dining room from the hallway.

Jimmy jumped up from the table, pushing the chair back with a squeak. "It's impossible to capture me Hollywood masculinity in words."

"Don't ye go comparin' yerself to Douglas Fairbanks, now," Mary said, patting Jimmy's cheek before kissing it lightly. "Ye need to learn to grow a mustache first. Then we'll talk."

Bridie looked at Anna. "Who's Douglas Fairbanks?"

"The man the Lord spent the most time perfectin'," Helen called from the kitchen.

Anna tried not to laugh. She had to remind herself often that Bridie had only been in Philadelphia for two weeks and still had a lot to learn about popular American culture. It went far beyond local theater put on by men after one too many whiskeys.

"I'll take ye to the pictures when his new film comes out next month," she promised.

"Well anyway, Mr. Higgins, it's a pleasure to meet yer acquaintance," Bridie said, sticking out her hand like she was closing a large business deal.

Jimmy returned the handshake heartily. "The pleasure is all mine, Miss Bridie. And please, call me Jimmy. Is that Miss Mary's dress I recognize on ye?"

Bridie gave her pink chiffon dress a twirl. "Since I traded all me clothes on the boat, I had nothin' to wear, and—"

"Why don't we all sit down and eat before supper gets cold?" Anna asked, posing the question as more of an order.

Sitting back down, Jimmy folded his hands on top of the table. "Marvelous idea, Miss Anna! I'm hungrier than after fastin' for Good Friday."

Protestants didn't fast on Good Friday. Anna squeezed Jimmy's shoulder tightly. "Wonderful. I'm goin' to grab the lemonade."

She hurried into the kitchen to find Helen and Theresa giggling over the poorly sliced pot roast. The pieces varied in thickness and size as if Theresa had cut it blindfolded. Anna should've known last year's mutilated Easter ham wasn't a one-time incident. But it didn't matter. They were serving a Protestant. Anna pushed Helen aside with her right hip and grabbed the roast without saying a word. Walking back into the dining room with a tight-lipped smile, she placed the heavy dish in the middle of the table.

Helen and Theresa exited the kitchen behind her with the brown bread and the lemonade, their expressions calm. Anna pushed aside the potatoes and green beans to make more room. It was still too crowded for her liking, almost confining.

"Do ye want me to move the flower vase?" Theresa asked, reaching across the table.

Anna swatted away her hand. "No, don't touch anythin'. Let's sit down and say grace."

The room was silent.

Anna bowed her head and made the sign of the cross. "Bless us, O Lord, and these, thy gifts, which we are about to receive from thy bounty. Through Christ our Lord. Amen."

She opened her eyes and made the sign of the cross again. Her sisters had joined in the prayer, as expected. Jimmy hadn't. He didn't know the words to the prayer. The others didn't seem to notice. Did Protestants even give thanks to the Lord for supper? She doubted it.

"Lovely grace, Anna. Can ye send over the bread, pleease?" Mary asked.

She nodded and passed the basket. Silverware clanged against dishes as everyone filled their plates to the edges. Anna wasn't hungry, but she took a large portion of everything to prevent second helpings from lengthening the dinner unnecessarily. The secret burned on her tongue.

Jimmy cleared his throat. "Miss Bridie, how's that head injury healin' up?"

Bridie held up her pointer finger while she swallowed. "Dr. Burns says I'll have a scar for some time, but me head's not throbbin' anymore. I get to take off the bandage next week, thank goodness."

"That's grand! I'm sure it'll disappear before the weddin', and ye won't have to worry about it showin' up in the photographs."

Mary elbowed Jimmy in the ribs. "It doesn't matter if ye have a scar or not. Ye're goin' to look just lovely," she said, grabbing Bridie's hand atop the table.

"I know we're all over the moon ye're engaged to be married, but Mary mentioned ye don't know yet where the weddin' will occur." Helen slowed down her last few words.

Anna stared at her plate. She folded and unfolded her damp hands in her lap. Of course, Helen had to start supper with an intrusive question. Would the others notice her reluctance to speak? Anna always controlled the direction of conversation, but maybe they'd see it as a graceful bow to Mary and Jimmy's celebration. Keeping quiet was the right thing to do. Mary couldn't know. None of them could know.

"Ah yes, well, we've been thinkin' it over…"

Helen placed her elbows on either side of her plate and leaned her chin on clasped hands. "Mary's been a member of St. Columba's since she arrived, but I suppose ye want to have the ceremony in yer own parish?"

"Where do ye attend Mass again?" Theresa asked.

"It's on the other side of the city, right?" Bridie echoed.

Anna twisted her linen serviette on her lap, keeping her eyes down. Her heart beat through her whole body, its vibrations stronger than the Wanamaker pipe organ's at Christmas. They couldn't know. Not here, not now. After supper. When Jimmy left. And they were alone. Just Mary.

"We haven't made a final decision yet because me parents are comin' over from Mayo, and they're bringin' me uncle, who officiates the best ceremonies I've ever seen. I wasn't sure if he'd be able to step in at St. Columba's and hold a weddin' so soon without talkin' to Father Lange."

Anna stopped twisting the serviette. She looked up at Jimmy, her mouth slightly ajar like she wanted to speak, but she couldn't find the words. Was he lying? Mary couldn't spend the rest of her life with a liar.

Helen clapped her hands. "What a wonderful surprise! I didn't realize—"

"I saw ye walk into a Protestant church today."

Everyone glanced at Anna in confusion. Mary tilted her head and turned to Jimmy, who kept his eyes locked on Anna.

"Ye were holdin' a package and walked right in, smilin'."

Jimmy shook his head. "Miss Anna, I don't know if ye were followin' me, but I promise ye I'm not a Protestant."

"Why didn't ye say grace before supper?"

"I like to say me prayers silently to meself."

"Why don't ye go to Mass every Sunday with Mary?"

"I've got a delivery route Sunday mornings. She knows that."

"Why did ye go into that Protestant church?"

"I was deliverin' a package from Wanamaker's for me good friend, James. He asked me to pick up a gift for his wife, who directs the children's choir at the church."

"Why...why..."

"Miss Anna, I'm not a Protestant. I was raised a good Catholic boy. While I haven't been to Mass in many months, I'm still Catholic. Not an active parish member, but still Catholic. And Mary and I will be married in a Catholic church."

Anna sat back in her chair. The secret dissolved blandly like a host on her tongue. She had been completely wrong, made insulting assumptions about poor, kind Jimmy. How could she have gotten herself in this mess? She had sinned more in a single day than in the last year. The Lord would certainly strike her down if she didn't go to Confession first thing tomorrow morning. Helen needed to come with her because her investigative spirit inspired the original temptation to follow Jimmy. She had sinned secondhand, always encouraging Anna to honor curiosity when it struck.

She took a deep breath and looked up at the ceiling, then let her eyes settle on the top of Jimmy's head. "I'm sorry, Jimmy. I …I thought ye'd been lyin' to Mary. I understand if ye don't want to invite me to the weddin' anymore."

Jimmy chuckled. "Nonsense. Miss Anna, ye should know better. If I was a Protestant, Mary wouldn't have anythin' to do with me!"

The sisters joined in laughter one by one, breaking the tension of the false accusation.

"If there's any secret-keepin' in the house, it's comin' from us," Jimmy said, wiping his forehead with a handkerchief.

He looked at Mary and nodded. Mary glanced at each one of her sisters and landed on Anna.

"I've been meanin' to tell ye all for almost a month now, but I couldn't bring meself to do it with Bridie's arrival and her startin' a new job and everythin'…"

"Mary, what's goin' on?" Bridie asked, a slight quiver in her voice.

Helen stood up. "Mary, are ye with child?"

Mary's eyes widened. "No, no, no. I'm not pregnant. It's just that—"

"Were ye with child?" Helen asked, still standing.

Mary sighed. "I was never pregnant. No one has died. We're not ill."

"What is it, then?" Theresa whispered, her eyes glistening.

"We're movin' to Pittsburgh after the weddin'. Jimmy's received a job offer."

The tension in the room would've been lighter if Jimmy had been a Protestant.

CHAPTER 9

AN UNEXPECTED REACTION

No one said anything for a moment. Silence reigned harder than at Holy Hour after six o'clock Mass on Sunday mornings. Anna didn't know whether to cry or beg or cuss. The Lord not only wanted to punish her for accusing Jimmy but also her sisters for whatever sins they'd committed and haven't repented for. He was taking away their Mary so soon after Bridie's arrival. How could they deserve that? They went to church every week and worked hard to send money back home to Listowel. They were finally together, the Galvin girls. One family.

"Where's Pittsburgh?" Bridie asked, breaking the silence.

Jimmy reached his hand to Bridie's resting on the table. "It's a beautiful city in western Pennsylvania. Two rivers join at the city's center where ye can go swimmin' and sailin'."

"I'd love to come visit on me day off at the salon. How long does it take to get there?"

"Yer whole day off," Helen said, walking away from the table into the kitchen. Theresa got up and trailed behind her without saying a word.

Bridie sniffed and pulled her hand away from Jimmy's and placed it on her lap. Anna knew the distance between the cities was greater than traveling to Dublin from Listowel. They'd be lucky to go a couple times per year on holiday, but she wasn't sure if Mary fully understood that. She was the most optimistic of them, always believing the good fortunes of the gypsy she visited once per month. Anna disapproved of such things.

"I'm sorry I didn't tell ye sooner. We wanted to wait until the offer was finalized," Mary said.

This was the first major decision Mary had made without speaking with her first. Now that she and Jimmy were officially engaged, Anna's opinion was no longer needed. It didn't matter that she had spent a year saving up enough money to buy Mary's passage to New York and cover six months' rent, so they didn't have to live in a boardinghouse. It didn't matter that she had stayed by Mary's bedside all night while Dr. Burns ran between their house and his, trying to cure the scarlet fever outbreak in half the neighborhood. It didn't matter that she had listened dutifully to all Mary's doubts and concerns while courting Jimmy. It was clear. Mary relied on Jimmy now, not her.

"I just got here, though! Why do ye have to leave so soon?" Bridie cried.

Mary stood up and wrapped her arms around Bridie from behind. Anna shut her eyes and a couple tears spilled without her permission. She felt like she was breathing in smoke.

"Jimmy got promoted and has some family in Pittsburgh he misses dearly. We'll only be there for a short time, and then we'll move back to Philadelphia before ye even miss us."

"Miss Bridie, this is an opportunity to give yer sister the life she deserves. Don't ye want that?"

Anna opened her eyes, her vision blurry. She blinked away her sadness, leaving hot, dry anger.

Bridie lifted her head and nodded. "Of course, I want her to be happy, but it feels like ye're takin' her away from me. I haven't seen her in four years."

Mary leaned over Bridie's shoulder to look at her squarely. "We're still goin' to be together. No ocean separates us anymore, just a lot of farms. Ye can telephone me anytime ye want and tell me all the gossip from O'Hara's."

"I suppose that's not too terrible. Ye better be sittin' by the telephone every day at seven o'clock. If ye miss just one call, I'll tell Jimmy to mail me one of yer favorite hats."

"If he dares, I'll have Anna mail me back all of the dresses I planned on leavin' ye," Mary said, trying to tickle Bridie under her neck.

Anna crossed her arms. "Mind ye, I will have no part in yer shenanigans."

Mary looked up from Bridie squirming in her seat. "Anna, what's got yer knickers in a twist? I'm just tryin' to cheer her up."

"About what? That ye're movin' hours away and we won't see ye except Christmas and possibly a summer holiday? That ye're gettin' married and uprootin' yer life away from us in the same month? That ye kept a secret for weeks that would affect us all? Now that Bridie's arrived to fill yer place in the family, ye're just goin' to leave and build yer own closer to Jimmy's. We're all we have. We have no other family. We're the only Galvins from Listowel livin' in Philadelphia. How could ye just leave without askin' us first? Are a few extra dollars an hour really worth leavin' yer sisters? I don't think so, and I thought ye didn't either until now."

Anna left the table without looking at Mary, taking her full plate with her. She entered the kitchen and dumped the plate into the sink, the clang deafening in the silence she left behind. She didn't wince. Helen and Theresa looked over from the corner where they stood conversing softly. Their cheeks glistened with tears. Anna nodded once, then passed by to the back door into the alley. She turned the knob and pulled it open but remained in the doorway when she heard footsteps approaching.

"Please don't leave, Anna. Please don't," Mary whispered.

Anna inhaled deeply, trembling. She shook her head, took a step forward, and tugged the door shut behind her.

CHAPTER 10

THERESA ENCOUNTERS HARRY GRANT

"Michael, come over here please!" Theresa called for the third time.

From the first evening she had helped Penny Grant put her three children to bed, Michael was absolutely enamored with her and listened to everything she said. But by the third visit, his obedient infatuation had deteriorated to indifference at her presence when he discovered she wasn't hired just to play with him. And now on the fifth visit, he turned to hiding in closets, changing locations each time she called him for bed.

Theresa still needed to change both George and Maggie's soiled nappies before they slept for the night. The dirtied ones needed to be boiled and dried by the morning. Michael could stay up longer reading his Jack and Jill books. She didn't have the energy to chase him down with a twin on each hip like the last time. Maggie had spit up five minutes after Theresa began bounding up and down the stairs in pursuit. The vomit-crusted blouse had yet to be washed.

The grandfather clock downstairs in the living room chimed eight times. Just another hour. Theresa usually enjoyed Thursday nights, but not this one particularly. Tomorrow marked one week since Jimmy Higgins came to dinner and Anna stopped speaking with Mary. None of them had taken the announcement about Mary and Jimmy's move to Pittsburgh after the wedding well, but Anna was absolutely furious. She didn't come back until after midnight, slipping in the back door. Mary grew fainter with worry every hour Anna didn't return. Eventually, Jimmy went home and Mary passed out from exhaustion in a dining room chair. Theresa still didn't know where Anna went all those hours. Anna refused to confess.

Bridie continued speaking with Mary, while Theresa decided to forgive her by the end of the weekend. They'd come to America to create their own lives, bigger than any they'd find in Listowel. Their mother hoped they'd achieve more than she ever did. The world was much larger than the two square miles they knew growing up. Theresa just wanted Mary to be happy, and besides, she wouldn't be there forever. Helen wasn't convinced, but Theresa swayed her under the condition that Mary made her the maid of honor. Bridie had taken the Pittsburgh news better than Helen's coveted new position, but Mary promised she could help assemble her bouquet. Anna had nothing to do with the preliminary wedding planning. She walked home every day from work by herself and went to St. Columba's after eating dinner alone in the kitchen. Family suppers ceased to exist.

And after coming back from church, Anna went right to sleep—just not in the bed she shared with Mary. She refused to sleep anywhere but on Helen's floor, even after Theresa offered to give up the double bed she shared with Bridie to squeeze into Helen's single bed. Anna played the martyr role so well that Mary started sleeping on the floor of their bedroom.

Theresa looked down at the babies lying side by side in their cradles. They cooed as she took turns giving the cradles a gentle push. She hummed the tune of a lullaby her mother used to sing before leaving her and her sisters to bedtime prayers. The words escaped her. *Fairy ... slowly ... lu la ...* Helen probably remembered them. She could recall every detail from her childhood—from the pattern of her Sunday dress that fit at eight years old to the name of the boy that pushed her in the River Feale after school. Theresa knew she missed home terribly. She continued to hum, the words starting to flow off her tongue like a traditional hymn.

"Fairy lullaby, me little child. Swing slowly in the cradle," she sang, her mother's words echoing in her mind. "Lu la lee, me little child. Close yer eyes, little infant."

The babies began whimpering with every flat note. Even though George and Maggie screamed more often than she'd like, and Michael rarely listened to her anymore, Theresa would rather be at Penny's than at home. Her sisters thought she was taking care of Mrs. McCormick's ill mother for a few hours. It wasn't a complete lie. She was in fact relieving Penny from children, but no one could know, especially not Anna.

She knew about Anna taking some of her money to invest in the market. Theresa didn't put her savings in the bank like her older sisters; she stashed it in a hatbox at the back of the shelf in her closet. Every time she received her wages, she took out the box and counted the original amount before adding more money. About a month ago, Theresa discovered two weeks' pay missing from the box. Anna said Theresa had one of her dresses in her closet and asked to rummage around to look for it that morning. Theresa chose not to confront Anna with the thought that she needed the money for something important. Anna looked out for her sisters.

Talk of a terrific market crash made Theresa nervous. She hardly knew anything about the economy, but the newspaper headlines spoke of a decline. Her coworkers at the factory discussed saving extra money for the holidays in case investments didn't make high returns. If Anna knew about her second job in general, she'd probably want the money to invest in the market since she made so much the first time. Theresa wanted to be cautious. If Anna found out she was working for Harry Grant, she'd be yanked to Confession every day for a month. Despite accusing Jimmy Higgins of being a Protestant, Anna took others' lying and sneaking around seriously. If only Theresa knew why she wanted the sisters to stay away from Harry.

"Theresa." Penny knocked on the doorframe. "I have to run over to a neighbor's house to pick up some sewing supplies I lent last week. I'll be back in a few minutes."

"I'll try to catch Michael while ye're out." She laughed.

Penny stepped into the bedroom and leaned against the powder-blue wall. "Don't waste your time trying…He's been refusing to go to bed until Harry gets home, which is at least another hour and a half on a good day."

Theresa nodded.

"I took him to the park today, and he ran around with some other boys, so I'm hoping he'll just tire himself out."

"Don't ye worry, I'll keep an eye on him while ye're out," Theresa said, waving Penny toward the door.

"Oh yes, I must go before it gets too late. Mrs. Bateman turns in quite early."

Theresa watched Penny scurry out of the room. She was again alone with the babies and her thoughts. Penny loved to chat, so she'd be gone at least a half hour. That gave her enough time to get all the nighttime chores done before she left at nine o'clock. Boil the soiled nappies, wash the dishes, fold the laundry, and put Michael to bed if she could manage. She glanced down at the babies, their cradles now still. George was asleep, but Maggie's gaze was fixed on the candle's shifting shadow cast on the ceiling.

The nappies needed to be boiled first, so Theresa picked up Maggie and brought her over to the bureau to change her. A blanket was already spread across the top, so she laid the baby down. Luckily, she wasn't quite old enough to roll over yet. Another couple months and Penny would need to put up rails. Softly humming to Maggie to distract her, Theresa lifted her dress and pulled off her bloomers, one chubby leg at a time. She didn't want George to wake because once one twin started crying, the other joined in like a duet.

Maggie didn't make a sound through her gummy smile as Theresa removed the smelly nappy and rolled it into a ball. The first time she changed Maggie's nappy, she almost got sick. It had been more than a year since she'd endured the horrific stench at home while watching infant cousins. Although it wasn't any more pleasant, the smell didn't bother her stomach as much with repeated exposure. Theresa wiped Maggie's behind clean and wrapped it in a new nappy. She sighed. George was next.

Theresa pushed the wrapped, dirtied nappy to the end of the bureau top and scooped Maggie up. She rarely fell asleep without a few minutes of bouncing. George hardly needed any coddling. He'd grow up to be an independent man, but different from Michael. One who would respect authority.

Theresa looked down at Maggie, whose eyes were still on the candle's flickering shadow. The boiling needed to be started before Penny returned. She prayed Maggie wouldn't start crying when placed in her cradle.

"Honey, I'm home early!" a deep voice announced from downstairs.

She froze. Harry Grant. Penny's husband. Anna's supervisor. The man who couldn't know she was there. She hadn't even heard the door open.

"I know you're up there...You better undress by the time I find you!"

Theresa placed Maggie back in her cradle and looked around the room for a place to hide. George woke up and began to cry. She wanted to soothe him, but she'd never see him again if Harry caught her.

Heavy footsteps started up the stairs, stopping intermittently.

Across the room was a small closet, but Penny usually kept it locked. Her breathing growing heavy, she raced over to it and tried to turn the doorknob. It was stuck.

"You'll find I'm excited to see you!"

Theresa yanked it back and forth with both hands. George's cries turned to screams. More footsteps.

"Honey, I want to run my hands all over your—"

Maggie started screaming along with George, drowning out Harry's seductive comments.

She tugged and twisted harder and finally the doorknob gave way. She threw open the door and shut it, encasing herself in complete darkness. Before her eyes could adjust, Theresa scrambled away from the door and backed into a stack of full boxes. The corner of the top box rammed between her shoulders, causing the entire pile to topple over on her. The weight of the boxes pinned her to the ground. She couldn't move.

The footsteps quickened across the floorboards and stopped in front of the door. The faint sliver of light coming underneath the door disappeared. George and Maggie continued wailing, but Harry didn't seem to pay them any attention from what Theresa could gather. He just stood in front of the door waiting. For her to move suddenly? For her to come out and lunge at him? Her stomach tumbled like the carnival acrobats that had come to the city in June. Was Harry…naked? She'd never seen a…It felt dirty to even say the word in her mind.

Something scratched the door.

"Are you playing hard to get in there?"

Theresa tried to push herself backward toward the wall, but the boxes were too heavy. She was trapped.

"I'm going to open the door on three."

She shut her eyes and nestled her chin to her chest.

"One…"

The babies' cries persisted even with their father in the room.

"Two…"

Was Michael still hiding in the other room? Had he heard anything? Would he give her away?

"Three!"

Harry threw open the door with such force that a lock of hair blew across Theresa's face. She kept her eyes closed for a few seconds, afraid of what she'd see. When she finally opened them, her gaze lined up exactly with what she didn't want to see. Her cheeks grew hotter the longer she looked at it. It was…bigger than she'd expected. Harry wasn't a noticeably tall man either.

He didn't seem to register that she wasn't Penny. He stood there, one hand still on the doorknob and the other dangling by his side, fingers spread far apart. Theresa glanced up to his face and back down to his feet. He just stared at her, his expression like he'd witnessed his wife give birth. Mouth agape, eyes searching, brow furrowed. Did he recognize her from the factory?

"Who…are you?" Harry asked, voice cracking.

Theresa said nothing.

"Tell me your name."

Again, she didn't answer. The silence felt longer than the time Father Lange dozed off between the homily and the profession of the faith in Mass. Theresa kept her eyes on the floor. Harry kept his attention on the top of her head but eventually remembered his naked state and swiftly bent to retrieve his pants. She watched him put one hairy leg in, then the other, and fasten the button. He left the belt hanging open.

Harry took a deep breath. "Are you going to tell me who you are? Or do I have to take you down to the police station?"

"I-I'm…I mean…"

"Spit it out, girl."

"Yer wife hired me to help with the children before bed."

Her words ran together like a child making a guilty confession. The truth came out so quickly that she didn't even consider lying. The Lord made her an honest woman, but then again, she didn't tell Penny about her job at the factory or Anna about her job with the Grant family.

Harry folded his arms across his hairy chest. "Penny hired you?"

"Yes, sir. She's been payin' me to come a few nights a week to assist her."

"How long have you been coming?"

"Not even two full weeks. She just wanted some help since ye come home so late."

He looked behind at George and Maggie, who had quieted down to a gurgle every couple minutes.

"Please don't fire me, sir," Theresa pleaded. If she ran into him at the factory, he would probably fire her there, too, despite not being her floor supervisor.

Harry uncrossed his arms and ran his fingers through his hair. "You have no need to fret. I'm not going to fire you. I only want to know where Penny has gone."

"She went over to a neighbor's not too long ago to fetch sewin' supplies."

He nodded and stepped forward into the closet, hauling the boxes off Theresa's body. She could breathe deeply again. Once the majority of the boxes were moved aside, she sat up and brushed the hair out of her face. Harry extended a hand to help her stand. Before she grasped it, he retracted it a moment to fix his belt, which he seemed to have forgotten to fasten. She watched Harry pull the pointed end of the belt through the buckle and adjust it to the appropriate size. Then, he slid the belt tail through his pant loops, making sure it lay flat.

Just next to the buckle, Theresa spotted two red stripes. She fixated on them for a moment, not realizing Harry had reached out again.

Harry cocked his head. "You say nothing about our meeting to her, understand?"

Theresa looked away from his belt and nodded, grabbing his hand. When she regained her balance, she brushed off box dust that had settled on her dress.

"Have we met before? You look awfully familiar," Harry said, stepping aside to give her space.

She tucked her chin to her chest and hurried toward the bedroom door.

"No, no, Penny and I met in a park and—"

"Are you sure? You resemble one of the workers on my floor at Apex Hosiery."

"I don't know of such a place."

"Interesting. I'll have to tell her the new nanny looks just like her."

Theresa swallowed hard.

Harry couldn't know that she and Anna were sisters or that she worked on the floor below them. She suspected that he and Anna had some sort of confrontation or that she knew important information that affected Harry if publicized. Anna kept her secrets to protect her sisters, but Theresa needed to know what happened between them. None of her sisters could find out about tonight. If Helen managed to sniff out her secret before anyone else, she'd assume Theresa was getting herself prepared to have children before marriage. Bridie wouldn't care much, other than the description of Harry's—lad.

Theresa continued through the door and walked around the corner to run downstairs before Penny returned. Harry chased after her and caught her hand as she landed on the top step.

"You don't have to leave. I'll go to the pub around the corner until the time I normally get home."

She still didn't look at him.

"I don't care if Penny hires you. I've been staying out too late, and it's the least I could do for her."

Theresa peeked out of the corner of her eye at his belt. The two red stripes. Her eyes narrowed.

"I have some business with a few pals anyway. They're bringing along some jewelry choices for Penny's birthday next week."

Jewelry. Bridie's locket. The assault. The men with the red stripes.

Harry waited for an answer. She needed him to leave immediately.

"Of course, thank ye, sir. I'll go find Michael now."

He nodded and passed her down the stairs, picking up his shirt on the way.

Theresa didn't know who the men with the striped belts were, but Harry was one of them.

CHAPTER 11

THE IRISH DANCE

The high, skipping notes of a single fiddle intensified when Helen opened the door to the community hall at the backside of St. Columba's. "The Silver Spear" was the only reel tune her older brother Mickey knew how to play on his tin whistle growing up. She could hum every note. These memories she wished would fade had stained her mind like red wine on a Holy Communion dress.

Helen hadn't been to the weekly dance in almost a month, but with Theresa's moping for the past two days, she saw it as an opportunity to liven up her sister. Every Saturday evening, the parish social committee hosted an Irish dance with live music, traditional dancing, and refreshments. She used to come regularly with Anna and Mary to admire the handsome men from afar, and if they were lucky, get asked to dance. Helen rarely fancied any of the men because they had two left feet, even while dancing a simple Shoe the Donkey.

She held the door open for Theresa, who lagged behind with a frown. Leaving the event feeling anything other than happy was impossible, but Helen knew the night would present a challenge. If something bothered Theresa, she only told her sisters once the problem had been solved. It would take an unholy amount of alcohol to get her to confess. Theresa's sullenness had added to the heavy silence in the Galvin household. Over a week had passed and Anna still hadn't spoken to Mary. She and Bridie were the only ones really conversing now, and the hair stylist couldn't stop gossiping about her latest client's burlesque days in the early '20s. By this morning, Helen had thought about tricking Bridie into taking a divine vow of silence at least three times. Unless Theresa started talking again by the end of the night, tomorrow might make it four.

She grabbed Theresa's hand and pulled her inside away from the entrance. An accordion, tin whistle, and bodhran joined the fiddle in a lively rendition of "The Banshee." Couples danced four-hand reels scattered around the center of the room while others chatted in groups along the walls and clustered around the refreshment tables. Her mother would've joined the dancing as soon as she stepped into the hall. She taught all her children to dance in secret when their father left the house. Once she rolled up the living room rug, the dancing and clapping began. A lump formed in Helen's throat.

She recognized the regular attendees, but a good portion of the crowd appeared to be newcomers, some clearly not Irish by their tanned skin. The overwhelming number of attendees tonight were young men. She and Theresa would have no problem finding dance partners for the evening.

"I'm feelin' rather woozy, so I'm goin' to get meself a drink," Theresa said, pointing to the back corner.

Helen didn't want Theresa isolating herself already. She knew plenty of people here.

"Why don't ye come over with me to talk to Mira Jameson? I see her just over there. We can get the truth on how Bridie's been gettin' on at the salon these past couple weeks."

Theresa shook her head. "I don't want to seem disinterested in the conversation, so I'll join ye after I've had a drink."

"That's fine, but don't go walkin' off anywhere now. We're here to have fun." Helen winked.

She watched Theresa walk over to the refreshment table and timidly wait for one of the women serving drinks to notice her. With her arms crossed, she kept looking over her shoulder at Helen and glancing toward the hall entrance. Was she expecting someone to arrive?

"Helen, darling!" Mira Jameson called, running toward her with arms open for a hug. They exchanged a tight embrace, and Mira pulled back to gaze at her like they hadn't seen each other in years. It had been a week.

"What are you doing here? I thought you stopped coming to the dances altogether!"

"Oh, ye know I couldn't stay away too long from the fellas." Helen laughed, gesturing to the multiple men eyeing them.

Mira giggled and lowered her voice. "I've been engaged in conversation all evening, some I wished to escape within the first thirty seconds."

"Ye and everyone in this room!"

"Did any of your beautiful sisters join you?"

Helen peeked back at Theresa standing in the corner holding a glass of water. "That one over there won't socialize. She's been awfully quiet the last two days, eatin' in her room and walkin' home alone from work. I can't figure out why. I thought bringin' her would cheer her up."

Mira took Helen's hands and gently swung them side to side. "I'm sure whatever's bothering her will pass. You said she was taking care of Mrs. McCormick's mother? Maybe the woman said something nasty to her. I heard she's grown quite senile in the last few months."

"Ye're right. She got quiet after she came home from Mrs. McCormick's on Thursday night. We'll see if she returns next week."

"Well, you know who won't stop talking?"

"Ye mean gossipin'?" Helen laughed.

"Bridie is an absolute doll. She's such a fast learner and obviously talented."

"Ye're tellin' me high-class American women find her charmin'?"

Mira tilted her head and looked up at the ceiling. "Well, I find her charming and a handful of customers do, too. Others find her…a bit irritating because she asks too many questions. At first, she didn't talk at all, but then something changed in her."

Helen wasn't surprised at all. Bridie's eagerness could be misconstrued for nosiness. "What kinds of questions?"

"When an older client started talking about her daughter's new fiancé, Bridie asked whether the man had enough money to support their lavish lifestyle."

Helen gasped. The nerve that child had! "I'll need to have a stern talkin' with her about askin' about people's wealth. She's set on livin' a life of luxury."

"Darling, she's only sixteen. She'll realize soon enough that unless you're born with money, you have to live vicariously through the society pages."

Out of the corner of her eye, Helen spotted a handsome man approaching them. He wasn't particularly tall or well-dressed, but she immediately noticed the squareness of his face, accentuated by the middle part in his slicked-back hair. His wide-set eyes stayed focused on her, and his steps matched the tempo of the slow jig playing. The closer he got, the bigger his smile became.

Mira pushed Helen forward, almost right into the man. He opened his arms to catch her, but she stopped herself before bumping into him.

"You don't want to dance with me?" he asked, rolling his shirt sleeves up.

Helen smoothed her hair and looked back at Mira, who gave her a stern expression.

"I'd love to dance with ye, but I only dance with men who properly introduce themselves."

The man waved his hand and bowed like she was royalty. "My name is William Rush, but I go by Bill."

Helen curtsied in jest. "It's a pleasure to meet ye, Bill. Is this yer first time comin' to a St. Columba's dance?"

"I just moved in down on North Bonsall Street and heard this is the place to meet lovely people like yourself."

"How wonderful! Me sisters and I live on North Bonsall. We're always walkin' up and down the street, so we're bound to run into each other."

"Pardon me, I'm terribly rude. I didn't ask your names," Bill said, motioning to both Helen and Mira.

Mira didn't say anything for a moment, so Helen introduced the two of them.

"Now that we've moved past formalities, may I interest you in a dance, Helen? I'm quite good at the Walls of Limerick."

She smiled at his knowledge of traditional dance as an American, but something more pressing caught her attention. Theresa was missing. She no longer stood in the corner next to the refreshment table. Helen glanced around the room, turning in a full circle. She wasn't dancing or conversing or eating. She wasn't sitting at a table or standing alone. Theresa wasn't in the hall.

"I'm sorry, but I seem to have lost sight of me sister and have to find her."

"Is something wrong with her?" Bill asked, his eyebrows furrowed.

"Well, she promised to meet me over here after gettin' a drink, and I think she might've left without tellin' me."

Mira placed a hand on Helen's shoulder. "Darling, why don't we go outside to see if she's getting some fresh air? It's rather stuffy in here anyway."

"I agree. Theresa was feelin' woozy, so fresh air might've done her some good," Helen said. She looked from Mira to Bill. "Please excuse us. I should be back in a few moments once we find her."

"I'll accompany you both, just in case something goes awry. Two lovely ladies like yourselves shouldn't be going outside alone at night."

Helen nodded and took Mira's hand as they walked toward the entrance, Bill following behind. She pushed open the door with her side and immediately spotted Theresa forced up against a wall by two men dressed in all black who didn't seem to be at the dance. She broke free of Mira's grasp and bolted toward her sister.

"Get away from her!" she screamed.

The men looked at Helen for a second, then ran into the unlit alley behind the church. Theresa walked toward her slowly, tears streaming down her face. Helen threw her arms around Theresa, hugging her tighter than when she walked into their North Bonsall home for the first time a year earlier. The two breathed heavily into each other's shoulders, Helen's blouse dampening with Theresa's tears.

After a moment, Helen pulled back and gently lifted Theresa's chin. "What happened? Are ye hurt at all?"

She shook her head but didn't say anything. Helen wiped away the remaining tears with her sleeve. Theresa's cheeks were flushed like she'd run all the way home and back. Her hair was somewhat frizzy, but she otherwise appeared to be untouched.

"My darlings, are you both alright?" Mira asked, approaching them.

"I would've beat them up for you," Bill added, looking at Theresa, "but your sister scared 'em off before I could even cuss at them."

Theresa let out an almost silent laugh. "Thank ye, sir."

Helen sighed. "She's unhurt, thank the Good Lord. But those scoundrels got away."

"What did they want? Were they attending the dance?" Mira gestured to the alley.

"I came outside to get some fresh air because I was gettin' rather dizzy inside with the loud music and talkin'," Theresa began softly, sniffing every few words. "Those men came up to me after a few minutes of standin' outside."

Bill scratched his head. "Were they lurkin' nearby, or did they just come up to you?"

"They came from the alley, so I didn't see them comin'."

"What did they say to ye?" Helen asked, her voice cracking.

Theresa shrugged. "Nothin' that made sense. They were lookin' for someone else and mistook me, I suppose."

"I'm so sorry, darling," Mira said, giving Theresa a side hug.

"I think it's best if I walk both of you home. I know Helen wanted some excitement this evening, but I think you've had more than enough," Bill said.

Helen didn't argue with him. She hated walking alone after dark, and with those dangerous men on the loose and Theresa vulnerable, they needed protection.

Bill looked at Mira. "Are ye comin' with us or stayin' at the dance?"

"I live in the opposite direction of North Bonsall, so I'll have a friend walk me home. I'll make sure to warn others inside."

Helen hugged Mira and waved as she headed back to the event.

"Ready?" Theresa asked.

"Oh yes, let's get ye home safely in one piece. The last thing I need is Anna gettin' angry with me for bringin' ye to the dance and ye endin' up like Bridie."

Bill looked over at Theresa. "What happened to this Bridie?"

"She...just hit her head and ended up with stitches."

"That's terrible! I hope it was only an accident."

"Yes...I believe it was an accident."

Helen glanced over her shoulder as they walked away from the church. She couldn't shake the feeling that more happened between Theresa and the men than she let on.

CHAPTER 12

BRIDIE'S NEW BEAU

───

"Bridie, darling, can you take the rollers out of Mrs. Ericsson's hair, please?" Mira asked, opening the front door of O'Hara's.

It was almost five o'clock. When the men started gathering outside the salon, Bridie knew the time had come to close up. Many of the stylists' beaus waited to walk them home after work. She watched them through the display window, talking to one another and laughing in between drags of their cigarettes. They all looked the same to her. Tall trousers, pressed button-downs, shiny Oxfords, crooked fedoras, greased hair. They all smiled the same way, spoke the same way, treated women the same way.

Bridie was quite shocked when Mira left a client in the middle of styling for the first time. She was a wonderful supervisor but a terrible flirt. Although she only chatted with the men for a few minutes, they flocked around her like pigeons in the park. Her vibrant blonde hair and contagious smile were enough to get every man's attention, even the ones going steady with other stylists inside. She called them "her darling boys," but Bridie couldn't understand why she needed a dozen pairs of wandering eyes on her when she had a fella. He just worked late nights.

"Of course, I'll finish her up," Bridie hollered back.

She'd never spoken with the men. At first, her hideous bandage kept her hidden in the back of the salon this time of day. And then, her healing scar kept her back when the bandage came off. But as she observed the men day after day, she realized they weren't anything special, not like Jimmy with Mary. The men laughed at Mira's wild flirtations and witty jokes, but she once overheard several make lewd comments about Mira's slim figure. Her jealousy of Mira's effortless attraction dissolved.

The other stylists tidied up their stations as Bridie removed the curlers from Mrs. Ericsson's hair. She had been checking the general appointment book when Mira took her break. A few women had requested her specifically since beginning at the salon, but not as many as she expected given how Mira and the other stylists praised her skills. It was strange, really. She was always pleasant and had grown quite conversational over the last week. Rich women loved talking about themselves. Mira had hinted she wasn't asking appropriate questions. What was so wrong with inquiring about their spending habits? They flaunted them, regardless.

"Sorry you don't have anyone to walk you home again, Bridie." Samantha snickered as she passed by on the way out the door.

Bridie ignored her as she continued unwinding the rollers. Samantha was the only stylist who purposely tried to make her day miserable. Some of the others ignored her, but no one else made snide remarks. Samantha pretended to mingle with the men, but she walked home alone. Bridie didn't feel any pity for her. She deserved to walk home alone and realize how much penance she needed to do to win the Lord's favor back.

Soon enough, she removed the last curler from Mrs. Ericsson's hair. Bridie glanced out the salon window. Mira was still talking to the men, only the crowd had shrunk significantly because the remainder of the stylists had left the salon. Mira often volunteered to close up to stay chatting as long as possible, which meant Bridie couldn't go home until Mira came inside to lock the door. Mrs. Ericsson left content, leaving her alone to tidy up everything the others missed. She didn't mind, though, because she liked the responsibility. Getting the salon ready for the following day gave her a sense of purpose.

Bridie looked around the salon. The floor needed to be swept. Stray hairpins and dust balls collected around the bases of chairs and in corners. She grabbed the broom from behind the permanent wave machine and first brushed around the chair where Mrs. Ericsson sat. Humming a psalm to herself, Bridie became entranced in the rhythmic whooshes of the broom. She moved from one chair to the next. She understood why Anna loved sweeping the house so much. It was soothing, something she could control. She'd felt out of control since arriving in America. The attempted robbery, the fall on the first day of work, Mary's moving to Pittsburgh.

A succession of hesitant knocks interrupted Bridie's thoughts. She looked up from the floor toward the front window. The crowd of men was gone, along with Mira, but one stood peering through the fingerprinted glass. Was he looking for someone in particular? She knew Mira would be back in a moment, so Bridie motioned for the man to come in. No one had locked the door or flipped the hanging sign from *open to closed yet*. He gave a toothy grin in acknowledgment and stepped inside the salon.

She noticed almost immediately the stranger's disheveled appearance. The men who typically waited outside the salon never had a hair out of place. His suit jacket was misbuttoned as if he'd dressed himself in complete darkness. One shoe was untied, the laces frayed like a girl's braided pigtails after playing outside. Even more strangely, the bottoms of his pant legs were cuffed to reveal bright red socks. The only tidy part of his appearance was his neatly shaven face. Without a single strand of facial hair, the man's pointed nose protruded a little too much for her liking.

"How can I help ye?" Bridie asked, clasping her hands behind her back. She bit her lip to avoid laughing. He was as unkempt as the drunkards she saw leave the pubs when she walked to work at seven o'clock in the morning.

The man took off his black hat with his right hand, smoothed his hair with his left, and placed it back on his head.

"Miss, I was wonderin' if ye knew of any reasonable barber shops near and about this area."

"One is down the street run by a man named Robert Callahan. Are ye not familiar with this part of the city?"

"Oh, I'm positively familiar. I live a few blocks over. I just wanted to get an expert opinion, since ye're a stylist and all."

She narrowed her eyes and tilted her head. Something was different about this man that she liked but couldn't put a finger on.

"Do ye think I'd do a mighty fine job cuttin' and stylin' a man's hair?"

"Ye would probably make a few mistakes in the beginnin', but who's to say ye couldn't?" he said, sticking his hands in his pant pockets. "Me name is Neil McGarry. It's a pleasure to meet ye…"

"Bridget's me given name, but I'm called Bridie."

"And where do ye hail from, Bridget called Bridie?"

She rolled her eyes at the grinning jokester. "I lived on a dairy farm right outside Listowel in Kerry."

"That's a lovely town. I've been there once meself when I was a boy," Neil said, taking his hands out of his pockets. He lifted his hat again and ran his fingers through his hair.

"Do ye have family in Listowel?"

"No, I was there makin' a delivery with some of the boys that worked for me uncle's tool company."

"And what do ye do now?" Bridie asked.

"I'm a Bond Bread salesman."

Neil reached behind his neck and attempted to scratch his upper back. His misbuttoned shirt stretched, and one button popped off, falling to the tile floor. With the left side of his mouth turned up, he reached down and picked up the button. Bridie glanced at the sudden dimple that had appeared in his cheek.

"Oh, I'm sure yer wife can fix that in a jiffy—"

"I can't say I have a wife, Miss Bridget called Bridie."

"I'm rather surprised, I admit. A handsome fella like yerself must have dozens of ladies flockin' to yer door. Or I suppose ye're steady with someone special, right? Most men that come by the salon are courtin' somebody employed here."

Neil shrugged. "Not one I can call me own."

"Well, ye're not goin' to find one here. Everyone's already been taken." She laughed.

Bridie eyed the clock above the entrance and realized she'd be late for supper if Mira didn't come back soon. Helen would also be coming to accompany her home.

"I'm afraid I have to ask ye to leave. I've plans for the evenin', and I can't be a minute late."

Neil rolled up his right sleeve and looked at his watch. "Me goodness, yes. I'm sorry to take up so much of yer time. Thanks for the wonderful conversation. I'll see ye around the neighborhood, Bridget called Bridie."

He straightened out his jacket and wrapped one side over the other, securing it with a self-embrace. Untucking one arm to open the door, he turned his head and winked at Bridie before exiting the salon. She waved and watched him disappear down the street.

"Who's that, darling?"

Bridie jumped and spun around to see Mira standing with a hand on her hip, smirking. She had come in the back alleyway entrance without making a sound.

"Just a man." She grabbed the broom and resumed sweeping like the conversation had never happened.

"He won't be just a man to your sisters."

Bridie looked up from the floor. "Who says I'm goin' to tell them?"

- - -

The aroma of fresh brown bread engulfed Bridie when she pushed open the front door. Anna was baking. She hadn't cooked or baked since the night Mary and Jimmy announced their plans to move to Pittsburgh almost a week and a half ago.

"Is that brown bread?" Helen asked, coming up the steps behind her.

"I think so. Did ye know Anna was goin' to be bakin' tonight?"

Helen shook her head. "Not in the least. When I left this mornin', she and Mary still weren't speakin'."

Bridie frowned and turned back to the house, stepping inside the door. She knew everyone was now home from work, but no single sound met her ear. No singing, no laughing, no bickering. The house was rarely quiet with the five of them all together.

"Hello?" she called to no one in particular.

"I can smell the bread. Come out wherever ye're hidin'!" Helen yelled, shutting the front door.

A few bangs came from the kitchen. The oven door slammed closed. Some scuffling and whispering. Bridie walked down the hallway, glancing into the living room on the right. Nothing seemed out of place. She entered the dining room, expecting the same, but stopped in her tracks and gasped.

Helen quickened her pace to catch up. "What is it? What's happened? Has somethin' gone wrong?"

The dining room table was covered in dishes piled with steaming food. An entire roast chicken, boiled potatoes, green beans, turnips, cherry pie, Waldorf salad. Bridie had never seen so much variety on a single table. Did they have guests coming over? Was it some special occasion she and Helen had forgotten?

"Good evenin', me lovely sisters," Anna said, walking out of the kitchen with a basket of sliced brown bread.

Bridie exchanged a worried glance with Helen. Anna had been sullen just hours before, and now she was happier than a lark. What had occurred while they were gone? Did she and Mary make up?

Theresa and Mary entered the dining room, one carrying a pitcher of lemonade and the other a big pot of beef stew with peas and carrots. They set them down on the edge of the table and stepped back next to Anna.

"Ye know me and Mary haven't been seein' eye to eye lately on her decision to move to Pittsburgh right after the weddin'," Anna began, "but we sat down this afternoon and have settled our differences. I support her move under the condition that she and Jimmy spend their first Christmas as a married couple here in Philadelphia."

"And me movin' doesn't mean we're not a family. We'll always be a family—the Galvin girls. I'm just findin' me own happiness, somethin' Mother and Father wanted for each of us," Mary added.

Anna gestured to the table. "When Theresa arrived home early from work, we asked her to help prepare a feast to celebrate as a family."

"Where did ye get the money to pay for all this food?" Helen asked.

"I took some money from me stock market winnin', but we have more than enough left to give Mary the weddin' she deserves," Anna said.

Bridie pulled out the nearest chair and plopped down. "I'm absolutely famished after bein' on me feet all day, so let's sit down before the food gets cold!"

Her sisters nodded as they found their spots around the table. They passed around the dishes, using their own forks to guide large helpings onto their plates. Bridie took extra servings of potatoes and brown bread but skipped the turnips. Only Anna liked them.

Mary looked over at Bridie. "Do ye have any excitin' stories from today's clients?"

"Oh, I'm sure she's just got some more of that ridiculous gossip from the rich ladies who come to O'Hara's more than a couple times a week," Anna said before Bridie could answer.

Helen placed her elbows on the table. "I like hearin' all about it since I—"

"There's never anythin' excitin' really," Anna interrupted, shaking her head. "Listowel probably has more hullabaloo this time of year with the horse races and festivals."

"—never have anythin' happen to me."

Anna rolled her eyes. "Hush now, ye're bein' silly. The Lord gives what he knows ye can handle, and what ye can handle at this moment is passin' me some potatoes, please."

Bridie stayed quiet for the next several minutes, subconsciously tearing her brown bread into small pieces while her sisters engaged in their own conversations. Mary sat to her immediate right, telling a story about Jimmy to Helen and waving around a spoonful of green beans. To Bridie's left sat Theresa, who argued playfully with Anna about Father Lange's weight gain while attempting to cut a piece of roast chicken on her plate. No one paid her any attention.

Ever since Mary's announcement and the standoff with Anna, the novelty of her arrival and injury had worn off. Her head wound was now a healing scar that could be covered up. She had a new wardrobe, courtesy of Anna. Her job duties at O'Hara's had become mundane to her sisters. She was old news.

Bridie picked up her water glass and tapped the side of it with a knife. The others stopped talking as if Pope Pius had cleared his throat.

"I guess ye don't want to know what happened with the man that came by the salon today."

The sisters' eyes widened into the shape of communion hosts. None of them had ever heard her mention a man, not even one she found dull or outright disliked.

"A man? What kind of man? A good man? A handsome man?" Mary said, rising from her seat a few inches.

Helen hushed Mary and put a hand on her shoulder, guiding her back down.

Bridie began, "I was tidyin' up O'Hara's for Mira as usual, and he came a knockin' on the window—"

"Why did ye let a strange man in—" Helen started saying, but she stopped when Anna stared at her.

"As I was sayin', the man was wavin'. Of course, we weren't closed yet, so I thought I didn't want to send him off," Bridie continued. "He wanted to know if there were any barber shops near and about O'Hara's."

"Did ye point him toward Robert Callahan's?" Mary asked.

"She's too proud to tell him that," Theresa said, sitting back in her chair. "I'm guessin' she told him the entire city had not a single barber shop."

"I wasn't that harsh to the poor man. He was friendly and not at all bad lookin', if I may say so," Bridie said as she rose to reach for the basket of brown bread in front of Helen.

Helen swatted her sister's hand away from the rolls.

"Whatever happened to askin' for things instead of reachin' across the table like an orphan without manners?" she said, putting the entire basket into Bridie's grasp.

"I've got mighty fine manners, and the Lord knows it, too."

Bridie sat back down and put another slice on her already full plate.

"Did he tell ye his name? Is he Irish?" asked Theresa. She leaned forward in her chair and rested her elbows on the table.

"Jesus, Mary, and Joseph, please tell me he's not some Italian fella," Helen said. "They use too much hair oil."

"Ye're talkin' about Lorenzo Bianchi from Mass, aren't ye?" Mary laughed.

"Ye can see the entire congregation's reflection in his hair when he sits in the front pew." Helen picked up a dirtied serving spoon, held it out like a hand mirror, and pretended to fluff her curls.

"If Sister Elizabeth knocks over a candle again, his hair will be gone before the flames reach the beams!"

"God bless him. All me prayers would be answered!"

Anna shushed her snickering younger sisters, and they turned their attention back to Bridie.

"His name is Neil McGarry."

"Neil McGarry?" Anna repeated. "His name is Neil McGarry?"

"That's what I just said."

"I think I know this Neil McGarry," Mary chimed in.

"His name sounds awful familiar," Theresa agreed.

"Well, what do ye know about him?" Bridie asked, smoothing the linen serviette in her lap.

"He's the man who broke Saoirse McHugh's heart."

All the sisters looked at Anna, who hadn't said more than a few words the entire meal.

"Wasn't Saoirse McHugh that girl who sneezed as Father Lange placed a host in her mouth?" Helen asked, her voice just above a whisper.

Anna nodded like the poor girl had passed onto the kingdom of heaven. Bridie had met the girl once, but the incident happened before she arrived. The parish probably talked about it for weeks. When Bridie made her First Communion, she tipped the chalice too far forward and red wine spilled all over her white dress. Making any sort of scene in the priest's presence automatically provoked whispers and stares.

"Do ye know what occurred between the two of them? She's such a sweet to the wee ones cryin' durin' Mass," said Mary, digging into her potatoes again.

"He's a rotten bachelor, that Neil McGarry," Anna said, folding her hands. "Under all the smiles and jokes, he's a goin' to break yer heart when the next pretty gal comes skippin' down the street. And he's much too old for ye, Bridie."

"Well, just how old is he?" she asked, her voice higher than expected.

"Last I heard, he was twenty-four, which is eight years older than ye."

"Well, it's not like he's Harry Grant. Ye didn't warn me about any Neil McGarry," Bridie said.

Anna looked around at her sisters. "I don't care how handsome he is. Ye all need to stay away from Harry Grant. He's mixed up in some dangerous business. I heard it meself."

Bridie ignored Anna and crossed her arms. "Well, I didn't tell ye the story to get a scoldin' based on parish gossip."

"But if he comes to O'Hara's again, ye need to tell him ye're not interested," said Anna, raising her chin.

"I bet Jimmy knows dozens of kind, handsome fellas to set ye up with," Mary offered.

Helen nodded. "The Irish dance at St. Columba's on Saturday was overrun with men much closer to yer age."

Bridie ignored her other sisters and continued to look at Anna.

"I've never shared anythin' about a man, and the minute I do, ye believe I intend on marryin' him?"

"I was just warnin' ye about seein' a man we know will end up terribly," Anna said. She glanced at the others, eliciting a chorus of "mm-hmms."

"Ye've never shaken his hand, so ye can't make a judgment on gossip from old Mrs. Ryan. I know she's keen on tellin' ye everythin' she hears while out and about."

Helen, Mary, and Theresa exchanged glances and then looked at Anna, who laughed.

"I heard about Neil McGarry's reputation straight from Saoirse meself. We arrived on the same boat from Cobh together, so I know the girl well enough to take her word on this shifty man."

"Well, if he stops by a second time, ye can't stop me from talkin' to him. Ye're not me mother, and ye never will be!"

Bridie stood up from the table and walked out of the dining room.

"Can ye believe what…" Anna's voice trailed off as Bridie ran upstairs and into the bedroom she shared with Theresa. Falling face down onto the bed, she buried herself in the pillows and yelled her frustrations. They wanted her to be independent and earn a wage to contribute to the household, but they wouldn't let her talk to a man who finally intrigued her. Theresa was only a year older than her, so why didn't they treat her the same? There was no difference between sixteen and seventeen. They thought she was a child because of the locket. She needed to talk to someone else, someone who would understand her.

Bridie would pay Aunt Nellie a long overdue visit.

GALVIN FAMILY PHOTOS

Back Row: Archie McGowan, Patrick Morrin, Tom Galvin
Front Row: Theresa Galvin McGowan, Anna Galvin Morrin,
Kit Galvin

Left to Right: Mary Galvin Higgins, Kit Galvin, Anna Galvin
Morrin, Theresa Galvin McGowan, Bridie Galvin McGarry,
Helen Galvin Rush

Back Row: Archie McGowan, Theresa Galvin McGowan, Anna
Galvin Morrin, Patrick Morrin
Front Row: Helen Galvin Rush, Bridie Galvin McGarry

Left to Right: Mary Galvin Higgins, Theresa Galvin McGowan, Anna Galvin Morrin, Kit Galvin

Left to Right: Helen Galvin Rush, Anna Galvin Morrin, Patrick Morrin, Theresa Galvin McGowan, Archie McGowan, Bridie Galvin McGarry

Helen Galvin Rush and Bill Rush

Back Row: Mary Galvin Higgins, Helen Galvin Rush, Anna Galvin Morrin, Patrick Morrin, Theresa Galvin McGowan, Archie McGowan, Bridie Galvin McGarry, Neil McGarry

Back Row: Archie McGowan, Theresa Galvin McGowan, Helen
Galvin Rush
Front Row: Patrick Morrin, Neil McGarry, Bridie Galvin McGarry

Back Row: Helen Galvin Rush, Bill Rush, Archie McGowan,
Catherine McGowan, Pat Morrin
Front Row: Billy Rush, Eddie Rush, Edward McGarry, Grace
McGowan, Thomas McGowan, Archie McGowan, Jr.

CHAPTER 13

BRIDIE'S SECRET VISIT

—

The gray stone Victorian house sat on the only hill in the quiet, upscale neighborhood. Bridie walked by it three times, double-checking the street address Father had given her before leaving Listowel. Compared to the two-room thatched cottage she grew up in, Aunt Nellie's ivy-covered three-story house with a wraparound porch was a modern-day castle. The holly bushes lining both sides of the uphill walkway were shaped into perfect spheres, not a branch out of place. She mustered all her courage and started up the path, counting the number of bushes she passed. There were forty-six.

Stopping in front of the porch stairs, Bridie gazed up to the top of the house. Each of the windows had a different pattern of windowpane—diamonds, circles, crisscrosses. Her favorite was the top window next to the double chimney. It was a stained-glass portrait of a river with a little bridge connecting the two banks. The various blues and greens were dull so early in the afternoon, but she imagined with a candle sitting on the windowsill, they were more brilliant than a cathedral's.

She hadn't felt this nervous since getting on the ship at Cobh Harbor. Even though she had known exactly what to expect, Bridie was still frightened she'd fall into the water, enter the wrong class cabin, or even worse, lose her ticket. She had stayed with a family friend in town the night before but didn't sleep a wink. When the rooster crowed at dawn, Bridie was already awake, dressed, and ready to be out the door. All the courage she had talked into herself during the night dissipated when she saw the ship like a morning frost in the sun. Bridie was on her own like every sister before her.

Remembering the reason she came to Aunt Nellie's, she took a deep breath and walked up the stairs, sliding her hand along the wooden railing. Each step creaked under her light weight. The moaning floorboards picked up where the staircase left off, and Bridie prayed that Aunt Nellie couldn't hear her from inside. She needed more time to mentally prepare to meet her mother's younger sister, who had been shunned from the family for chasing an American man across the Atlantic. She and Father had been childhood friends before he married Mother, and he had kept in touch with Aunt Nellie through letters over the years without Mother knowing. Before Bridie left, Father took her aside and revealed his secret communication with Aunt Nellie.

She was initially shocked because Mother spoke about Aunt Nellie as if she were dead and told her children not to seek her out if they went to America. Mother didn't even know Aunt Nellie's whereabouts, so it would've been impossible to find her if any of them had the desire. Bridie knew few details about Mother and Aunt Nellie's falling out. But for some reason, Father wanted her to have the address in case she ever needed guidance or help. In the moment, Bridie took Father's gesture as an insult because she was perfectly capable of taking care of herself, especially while living with her four older sisters. Now standing at Aunt Nellie's door, she finally understood.

Bridie glanced down at herself. She looked presentable enough in Mary's Sunday best. When her sisters left for work this morning, they believed she had called out sick because of a fever and chills. The last they saw her; she was lying in bed with a cold compress on her forehead. As soon as she heard the front door shut, Bridie spent several hours picking out a reasonable outfit, pinning her hair, and covering up her scar. Then, she spent an additional hour figuring out which trolleys would get her across the city to Aunt Nellie's.

She looked around the porch and stepped closer to the door. Should she knock loudly? Would Aunt Nellie hear her if she were on the third floor? Did she have a butler that answered the door? Was anyone home at all? If she did come to the door, would she even want to talk to the daughter of the woman who exiled her from the family? Did Father even tell Aunt Nellie Bridie had her information and might visit? Coming here was a terrible idea. She didn't even know this woman. This woman didn't know her. They weren't family; they were strangers.

She spun around and started across the porch when the door opened.

"Pardon, but may I help ye?"

Bridie froze. The high, clear voice sounded eerily like her mother's.

"There's no need to be afraid. Do I know ye?"

She turned slowly, keeping her eyes down until she faced Aunt Nellie. The woman was the spitting image of her mother, except her hair was more auburn, like Bridie's, instead of mousy brown like the rest of her sisters'. It was braided and tossed over her shoulder. She wore a green chiffon dress with a hemline that hit right below her knees. She was barefoot and wore no jewelry except for a delicate silver pendant.

"Well, I...I'm Bridie Galvin and—"

Aunt Nellie gasped and covered her mouth with her hand. "Bridie Galvin? Me niece, Bridie Galvin?"

"Yes, me father gave me yer address before comin' over a few weeks ago and—"

"Oh, the mighty Lord is finally good to me!" Aunt Nellie cried, stepping forward and embracing Bridie.

She didn't know how to react, but eventually she relaxed in her aunt's tight grip. The woman smelled of lilac and tobacco.

Aunt Nellie stroked Bridie's hair and pulled back to look at her. "Yer father told me ye were comin' over, but I didn't think I'd ever get to meet ye."

"I wasn't plannin' on it until I ran into some trouble with me sisters." Bridie laughed.

"Let's move inside, and I'll fetch some tea. Do ye take milk and sugar?"

"Yes, ma'am, just as me mother does."

Her aunt smiled faintly but didn't say anything. She motioned for Bridie to follow her into the enormous house. The entryway was larger than her entire living room. A crystal chandelier hung from the vaulted ceiling just above the bottom step of a grand, curved staircase. The dark hardwood floor was so recently polished that Bridie could see a faint reflection of herself.

"Shall I take me shoes off?" she asked, not wanting to track in dirt.

Aunt Nellie shook her head. "Ye're quite alright. I just like the coolness of the floor under me bare feet. Ye can't take the farm girl out of me, I suppose."

"That's exactly what I want to do," Bridie said.

"Believe me, Listowel will never leave ye."

Bridie just nodded and continued following her aunt into a spacious sitting room decorated wall to wall with floral. The upholstered sofa was covered in pink roses, clashing with the throw pillows embroidered with daffodils. No two decorations or pieces of furniture had the same type of flower. The longer she looked around the room, the dizzier she became. She had been thinking about reading *The Secret Garden*, but this experience was enough.

"Me dear, please sit down, and I'll put on some tea. Take a look at the flowers around ye while I'm gone. I love them because they never wilt," her aunt said, gesturing toward her sofa on her way out of the room.

In the couple of minutes Bridie had spent with Aunt Nellie, she already felt more connected to home. Maybe it was free spirit or the nature-inspired decor. She didn't feel confined in this house, and it wasn't the size. The air held a quietude she hadn't experienced once in Philadelphia. Helen would love it here.

"I've got the kettle goin'," Aunt Nellie sang off-key, returning from the kitchen. She sat down in a yellow armchair across from Bridie.

"Thank ye for invitin' me in. I was rather uncertain whether ye'd want to see me or if ye'd even recognize me."

"Bridie, dear, ye've got me hair color and yer mother's complexion. Of course, I was goin' to recognize me own kin."

Bridie relaxed her posture, crossing one leg over the other. "Well, I guess I'll start by sayin' I don't know why Father gave me yer address but not me sisters. And I can't say I understand why ye kept in touch with him after ye left. And I'm not sure what I'm tryin' to get out of our meetin', but I—"

"Why don't I start by answerin' yer first two questions?" Aunt Nellie laughed, crow's feet appearing.

"Oh yes, that would be mighty helpful."

Aunt Nellie pulled the ribbon out of her hair and unwound her braid. "I'm sure yer father told ye he and I were childhood friends. We used to fish in the River Feale every mornin' before school started. We stayed close even when he began courtin' yer mother. They fell in love quickly, and I was so happy for 'em. Yer father and I were like brother and sister, never anythin' more."

"And when did ye meet this American fella?"

"Just before yer parents got married, I went down to Cork to visit a friend for a few weeks. She had family from America visitin' as well, and I happened to fancy her cousin Frank. He was a businessman in Philadelphia. We spent every moment of his holiday together, and he proposed I come with him back to the States. I was and still am a hopeless romantic, so I said yes, of course. But I knew I had to tell me family before leavin'. I'd never run off without sayin' goodbye."

Bridie uncrossed her legs and placed her elbows on her knees. "So…ye left without goin' to Mother and Father's weddin'?"

Aunt Nellie sighed. "Yes, that's exactly what I did. I was a terribly stupid girl. Yer mother was so angry that she swore she'd never speak another word to me. I don't regret comin' to America, but I regret when I left."

"Why wasn't Father angry like Mother?"

"Because he understood what it meant to be deeply in love. He loves yer mother more than anythin' in the whole world. And because I felt the same way about Frank, I needed to leave with him. If I didn't, I probably wouldn't have gone at all."

"So that's why ye've kept writin' all these years," Bridie said, looking at the ceiling and nodding. "It was yer way of knowin' the happenings in Listowel without goin' back."

"He informed me every time one of ye moved to Philadelphia. I've been longin' for the day I get to meet me sister's children, but I never wanted to interfere in yer lives because of what yer mother's probably told ye about me."

Bridie glanced down, ashamed at what she used to believe. "She said ye betrayed and abandoned yer own family for a two-timin' slick American."

Aunt Nellie shut her eyes and breathed in deeply. When she opened them again, a couple tears spilled out. She pushed her hair behind her shoulders. "Yer father never told me exactly what she said, but I'm not surprised. Frank was truly an upstandin' husband, but I did betray her trust."

"Now meetin' ye and knowin' Father was writin' ye this whole time, I believe she probably said that to prevent us from gettin' hurt the same way. But me sister Mary is gettin' married in a week and shortly after, she's movin' to Pittsburgh with her husband."

The kettle whistled from the kitchen, startling Bridie. Aunt Nellie held up her pointer finger and ran out of the sitting room. She returned less than a minute later with two cups of steaming tea on porcelain saucers. Both were decorated with multicolored roses.

"I hope ye don't mind, but I took the liberty of puttin' cream and sugar in it already," she said, her hand shaking while handing Bridie one of the cups.

"Not at all. Thank ye."

Aunt Nellie took a sip of tea, then placed the cup and saucer on the nearby coffee table. "So, yer sister's gettin' married? How splendid! Is anyone accompanyin' ye?"

"Well, I did meet a nice fella outside O'Hara's Beauty Parlor where I work, but when I told me sisters about him, they said I couldn't talk to him anymore because of his reputation."

"I know precisely how ye're feelin', dear. They're goin' to keep dislikin' him unless they meet him for themselves. I think ye should bring him to the weddin'."

Bridie raised her eyebrows. "Really? Wouldn't they get angry?"

Aunt Nellie bit her lip. "I suppose they'd be angry at first, but ye're tryin' to build a bridge by introducin' him."

"Anna's the one really against him, but I think gettin' them in the same room would ease her concern."

Aunt Nellie nodded and took another sip.

"Would ye be interested in comin' to the wedding, too?" Bridie asked, putting the cup and saucer in her lap.

The question escaped her lips before she realized the significance of the invitation. Her sisters didn't know Aunt Nellie lived in Philadelphia, nor did they know Father had been in contact with her since she left Listowel. They also didn't know Bridie lied about work to come visit her and believed her to be a deceitful woman.

Aunt Nellie sat up straighter. "Are ye sure? Do ye think they'd welcome me?"

Bridie trapped herself accidentally. "I...I think they would once they meet ye."

"Two surprise weddin' guests. What an excitin' day it will be!"

CHAPTER 14

MARY GETS MARRIED

Mary adjusted her Juliet cap veil for the fourth time in fifteen minutes. She'd seen the cloche style in a few fashion magazines and fell in love with how it sat on the models' heads, but she didn't realize how itchy the tulle would be on her forehead. No matter how she arranged her bangs underneath, the scratchy fabric still managed to bother her. By the end of the ceremony, she would certainly have an ugly red rash above her eyebrows.

"Stop touchin' yer veil, or I'm goin' to sew it to yer head!" Anna said, kneeling to fix the dress's frayed hemline.

Theresa walked from the back of the room carrying the bouquet of white roses embellished with silver tinsel and ribbon she'd spent the last three hours making. Putting together the bouquet was originally Bridie's job, but she gave up after not being satisfied with anything she made. Mary hadn't even been critical of a single one. Bridie was just too hard on herself.

"How does it look? Do ye like it? I can make any final changes ye want," Theresa said.

"It's absolutely exquisite. Thank ye." Mary reached out and took the bouquet from Theresa. The strands of ribbon hanging from between the roses had delicate pearls to match those sewn onto her cap veil and the bodice of her lace dress. She touched the pearl necklace at her collarbone Jimmy had given her as a present for courting a whole year. Every gesture he made had to be extravagant, but she wouldn't want it any other way.

Helen entered the back entrance of the community room of St. Columba's where they had been preparing since seven o'clock this morning for the wedding. It was a quarter to ten, and Bridie still hadn't returned from the secret errand she ran almost an hour earlier. Mary suspected Bridie was planning something. She hoped for a handmade present, but the gypsy she frequented had told her the past and the present would converge at her wedding. None of the sisters knew about the prediction. Anna sent Helen to look for Bridie and bring her back because she was taking so long, and Mary was starting to panic as more people arrived.

Anna stood up and placed her hands on her hips. "Did ye see any sign of her?"

"She's vanished completely. I went back to the house, stopped by the grocer's, and even checked O'Hara's. I also didn't pass her in the street goin' any of those places. Nobody has seen her," Helen said, a tremor in her voice.

Despite the prophecy, Mary couldn't believe Bridie would go missing at such an important time. They'd grown almost inseparable since her arrival, even though they weren't close back in Listowel. She let Bridie borrow anything from her closet, including from her treasured hat collection. She taught Bridie how to cover her scar with makeup when the bandage came off. She listened to Bridie's initial frustrations of working at O'Hara's. And now Bridie was gone.

She needed this day to go well, to be everything she'd ever dreamed. Jimmy would be standing at the altar, seeing her for the first time in her wedding dress. His parents and uncle came into New York yesterday afternoon and arrived in Philadelphia by train in the evening. Mary desperately wanted to meet them before the wedding, but Jimmy had insisted on not seeing each other until she walked down the aisle. Mother and Father couldn't make the trip because of the expense. Anna had sent over what she thought was enough money to pay for their ship fare. When they went to book their tickets at the last minute, they realized they couldn't afford the remaining second-class openings. Mary cried herself to sleep the night her mother broke the news in a letter. It had been four years since she saw them.

"Did ye hear that?" Helen asked, fluffing her hair in the mirror.

Anna shook her head.

A muffled knock sounded at the back entrance. Theresa jumped up from her chair. "Do ye think it's Bridie?"

"Why don't ye answer the door and find out?" Mary said, reaching to adjust her veil cap again.

Theresa sighed and ran toward the door, throwing it open with anticipation. Less than fifteen minutes remained until the ceremony was set to begin. Standing in the doorway was not Bridie but one of Jimmy's groomsmen and fellow ice delivery men, Arthur. He had sweat dripping down the right side of his face.

"Miss Mary, I've come from the front of the church to let you know people are starting to get antsy. You should be lining up in the lobby so we can start right on time. I think most guests have arrived," he said, placing his hands in his pockets.

Anna answered for Mary. "Ye see, Bridie's gone missin' for an hour now, and we're tryin' to wait until she returns."

"We can't leave the guests waiting too long after ten o'clock because Father Lange says there's another wedding happening at eleven. Everyone has to be cleared out by then."

"It might be best to move to the lobby and get ready, and that way we can look out for Bridie comin' down the street," Helen offered.

Theresa looked at Mary. "We can go around the buildin' and follow Arthur so nobody will see ye."

"I suppose I don't have a choice really," she said, gathering up her bouquet she had set down on a table. The wedding would go on whether Bridie was late or not.

As her sisters held her floor-length lace veil, Mary followed Arthur along the side of the church and around the front. She looked up and down the street for Bridie before going inside the lobby. No sign of her. The guests' chatter was loud through the closed double doors, but she couldn't make out any conversation.

Were they talking about how radiant she'd look? Or whether she and Jimmy made a handsome pair? Or how they'd like the wedding to start right now? She knew most of the guests because they were part of St. Columba's, but a handful were friends of Jimmy's.

The lobby air was stale yet humid. She could smell her own sweat above the dozen spritzes of homemade perfume Anna had given her. Lemon and lavender oils combined were pretty strong, but Mary needed at least three handkerchiefs tucked under each arm to really offset the other unpleasant scent.

"Alright, now that you're all here, I'm going to go back to Jimmy and tell him you're almost ready but waiting on

Bridie," Arthur said before opening one of the double doors into the church.

Mary made sure to stay behind the door so no one would get an early sneak peek of her dress. She pulled her cap veil forward. Her white satin heels were already pinching her toes. The stunning pieces of jewelry and clothing didn't feel like hers. She felt like she was trying on couture from one of Bridie's rich clients at O'Hara's. Is this how Bridie felt trading the locket for her clothes on the ship? Did she feel like a fraud? An Irish farm girl in disguise? Tomorrow she'd go back to not caring what others said about her because she'd feel like herself again without all the lace and pearls and flowers.

Helen put her ear up against the door. "The organ is startin' to play."

"If the Lord plans on this weddin' happenin' today, he'll bring Bridie back to us. And if he doesn't, I'll be havin' a stern talkin' with him in Holy Hour on Sunday," Anna said, opening the front entrance.

Mary sat down on the floor, not caring to move her veil aside. "I should've known where Bridie was goin'. She's been tellin' me everythin' lately."

Theresa knelt beside her and took her face in her hands. "I've been sensin' this past week that Bridie's been hidin' somethin' from all of us. It's not yer fault she's not here. It's hers, and she'll owe ye the sincerest apology when she returns."

"She's comin'! Bridie's comin'!" Anna cried, looking back and forth from the door to Mary.

Helen ran next to Anna. "Let me have a look! Is she carryin' anythin'? Is anyone else comin' with her?"

Anna squinted, then turned back to Mary. "She's got two people followin' her. A young man and an older woman. Did ye invite any more guests?"

"No, not that I'm aware of." She was almost certain that everyone invited had shown up. Mother and Father were the only ones who turned the invitation down because of the ship fare. Was the gypsy right? Were people she'd forgotten to invite coming?

"Oh, the Lord is testin' us today, Mary," Helen said, backing up from the doorway.

Mary moved to stand up but tripped on her veil, ripping a hole with her heel. Theresa gasped and touched the destroyed lace in disbelief. It couldn't be sewn back together in the few minutes before the ceremony, so Mary tried not to think much of it. The veil was so large that a small hole wouldn't be seen from the pews.

"Do ye know who the people are?" she asked, trying to stand up once more.

Helen peeked out again. "The man is definitely Neil McGarry. The woman, I'm not sure, but she looks awfully like Mother with red hair."

"Do ye think it's…" Anna covered her mouth.

Theresa went to the door to see for herself. "It can't be, can it?"

Anna nodded, mouth agape. "I think…I think it is her."

"We better get away from the door now. They're almost here," Helen said, pulling Anna and Theresa by the arms.

They gathered in front of the double doors at the back of the lobby, Mary in the middle, waiting for Bridie and her uninvited guests to walk in. None of the sisters spoke in the moment that passed. They kept their gaze on the entrance. When the right door finally opened, only Bridie stepped in and let the door close behind her. The others stayed outside.

"I'm so terribly sorry I took so long to run me errand. It was really important to me," she said, walking toward her sisters.

Anna stepped forward in front of Mary. "Isn't yer older sister's weddin' day important to ye? Don't ye think it's important to her?"

Bridie visibly shrank as Anna raised her voice with every word. "Of course. I just think there's some people we'd all want to meet and who wanted to be there for Mary's special day."

"Well, why don't ye bring them inside then if they're so important to ye?" Helen asked, pointing toward the entrance.

Without a word, Bridie turned around and opened the door, waving the two people inside. The woman entered first, who Mary still couldn't identify, then Neil McGarry. They were both dressed appropriately for the occasion, which Mary didn't expect from how her sisters reacted to their coming. The redheaded woman wore a blush pink dress and matching cloche, while Neil sported a well-pressed three-piece suit. He was more handsome than she remembered.

The woman stepped forward and placed a hand just above her left breast, admiring Mary's dress. "Ye look absolutely beautiful, Mary, dear. I know me comin' is quite a surprise, but I wanted to introduce meself. I'm Aunt Nellie, yer mother's younger sister."

Mary didn't know what to say. This woman had betrayed their mother, and Bridie somehow had the audacity to contact her and invite her to the wedding. She couldn't understand how or why. No one ever knew where Aunt Nellie ended up settling with her American husband. Did someone in the family stay in touch with her? Were Mother and Father lying to them? None of it even mattered in this moment because the woman was standing right in front of her, complimenting her like they were family.

Neil McGarry looked around the room, whistling softly. Mary didn't care much about his presence because she was more curious about him than she wanted to admit to Anna in light of her strong opposition. Bridie's choice to bring him without asking angered her more than who he actually was, unlike Aunt Nellie. She didn't understand why Bridie would do this. Was she trying to ruin the wedding? Mary could believe Bridie trying to steal the spotlight by making a better bouquet than Helen or wearing fancier shoes than Anna. But bringing guests to ruin her wedding? That seemed too far for even her. There had to be more to the story. She was her little sister after all.

The organ began playing louder. She couldn't waste any more time being upset about Bridie or Neil or Aunt Nellie. This was her wedding day to the love of her life, and nothing could ruin it. It was finally time.

"Bridie, please escort yer guests out of the church. We will talk about this after the weddin'. Ye will not stand near the altar, but ye may sit in the first pew," she said, her tone completely calm.

"Mary, please! I want to explain why I brought them!"

She touched her cap veil one last time and clutched the bouquet against her dress. Ignoring Bridie's plea, she turned toward the double doors and nodded to Anna and Helen to open them. She would soon become Mrs. Mary Higgins.

CHAPTER 15

THE CONFRONTATION

Bridie sat alone at a table in the back corner of the party. Almost an hour into the wedding celebration, no one had come to talk to her. Mary stayed attached to Jimmy's hip and didn't even turn a head her way. Her other sisters kept busy in conversation with all the guests, floating from one group to another. St. Columba's social committee had completely transformed the usually bare community hall into a wonderland of autumnal flowers and delicate paper cutouts in the two hours between the ceremony conclusion and the party commencement. The floral centerpieces were the only thing keeping her awake at this point. She picked up the mason jar full of pansies and sniffed it whenever she felt drowsy.

After the verbal altercation with Mary before she walked down the aisle, Bridie took both Neil and Aunt Nellie outside. She apologized for the unexpected escalation and the need for them to leave right away. She knew her sisters would be shocked by their arrival, but she didn't think Mary would be so upset she'd send them away. They agreed to leave without putting up a fight, although Aunt Nellie was rather disappointed and wished to meet with them again after they all settled down. Bridie guessed Anna and Mary would refuse to even be in the same room as Aunt Nellie again. Helen and Theresa could probably be convinced if she promised to give them each an appointment at O'Hara's without cost.

Loud applause and whistles woke Bridie from her daydreaming. An eight-hand reel had finished, and a tin whistle began an airy, light jig. Men and women paired up, arms wrapped around waists, and started skipping in a large circle in the center of the room. Every sixteen counts, they reversed direction. A few older couples didn't switch fast enough and created gaps in the circles, but they kept smiling and laughing at themselves.

Sighing, she looked around the room once more. The scene hadn't changed. Mary and Jimmy were holding hands and beaming. Theresa and Helen were speaking with Mira Jameson. Anna stood at the edge of the dance floor, clapping along to the beat. She wished to be that carefree today. She'd been looking forward to Mary's wedding since the engagement, growing giddier every day that passed like a child counting down to Christmas. It would be the first wedding she'd ever attended, since Mother and Father forbade any of their children under fourteen from going to community weddings. They believed young children distracted from the couple's celebration, much like uninvited guests, she supposed.

Neil McGarry had arrived.

Bridie spotted him leaning against the wall near the back entrance. How had he gotten in? Why did he return? Holding a gift wrapped in newspaper in one arm, he took a swig of beer with the other, tipping his head back to get the final drops in the glass. His hair was disheveled, a cowlick sticking up at the crown of his head, and his tie was pulled out from his vest. This was not his first beer.

She needed to get him out of here before anyone noticed, especially Mary. She stared at him, hoping to make eye contact and wave him down. Eventually, he noticed and grinned, lifting the poorly wrapped present to show her. He stumbled forward but luckily caught himself and the gift. Bridie motioned for him to stay where he was and scurried along the wall, weaving in and out of laughing people clinking glasses. She kept her gaze on Neil. When she finally reached him, he had slumped to the floor with his back against the wall and legs straight out in front. She crept down to his level and placed a hand on his knee.

"Mr. McGarry, what are ye doin' here? I thought I told ye to go on home?" She used her sweetest voice, which was usually reserved for Anna in her strictest moments.

He raised his eyebrows and pointed to himself. "Bridget called Bridie, what am I doin' here? Ye're really askin' me that? Ye're the one who invited me."

"I know I did, but then I requested ye go home because Mary doesn't want ye here." She tried to keep her voice low, but it was hard to hear with the music and chatter.

"Well, I wanted to come back because I forgot to bring me present last time."

Bridie held out her hands. "I promise I'll give the gift to Mary, and I know she's goin' to love it."

"I don't think so, Bridget called Bridie," Neil said, shaking his head. "I must give it to her meself to prove I'm not a bad man like yer sisters believe. I'd love to take ye to the cinema, but only with their approval."

She instantly regretted telling Neil what her sisters thought of him. Even when sober, he was pretty keen on proving his perceived reputation false and clearing his name. All in the name of courting her. Bridie knew she needed to start thinking before she spoke.

"How many drinks have ye had since I've seen ye?"

Neil counted on his fingers. "Four I think?"

"And why did ye have four drinks?"

"To give me the courage to stand up to yer sisters."

She glanced behind her to make sure no one had heard him. "Why don't we talk about this outside? I'll understand ye better. It's too noisy in here to plan our outin'."

He stroked his chin, thinking. "I'd rather see Mary first, maybe get another drink, and then go outside."

She sighed. This was going to be a lot harder than she thought. Where was Mira with her golden tongue when she needed her? Folding her legs underneath her, she sat on her behind and crossed her arms. As long as she stayed physically next to him, he wouldn't be able to approach Mary. Honestly, in his condition, he probably couldn't even stand back up.

"Bridie, what is the meanin' of this?" Anna whispered angrily into her ear.

Startled, she turned to see her eldest sister crouched over her, hands on her hips. Bridie had never seen so much white in Anna's eyes.

"Can't ye see I'm tryin' to get him out of here?"

"Was this yer doin'? His comin' back in this condition?"

Bridie shook her head, eyebrows raised to her hairline. "No, I'm just as surprised as ye! I'm tryin' to coax him to leave, so I don't ruin the weddin' even more."

Anna took her hands off her hips and knelt next to Bridie. In her most pleasant tone she said, "Mr. McGarry, I'm askin' ye to step outside. We need to talk about some things."

"Only if I get to speak with Mary and Anna." Neil spun his beer glass on the floor.

Anna chuckled. "Ye'll get to speak with Anna, don't fret."

Neil pulled in his legs and leaned forward to stand up. He tried to use the wall for assistance, but he had nothing to grip for support. Bridie grabbed Neil's arm and struggled to pull him up, but he was mostly limp. Finally, he found some stability on his feet and relied on the wall to keep himself standing. Bridie pushed open the back door and pulled Neil outside, not realizing that Anna had disappeared until the door shut.

"What are we doin' out here, Bridget called Bridie?" Neil asked, his words becoming increasingly slurred by the minute.

"We're goin' to talk about why ye came to the party, but we're waitin' for me sisters first."

His eyes widened. "Yer sisters? Will I get to meet Mary again?"

"No, but ye'll get to see Anna, Helen, and Theresa!"

Her sisters walked out the door just as she said their names.

"The Galvin girls! What a pleasure to see ye again!" Neil held up his hand as if toasting their arrival, despite leaving his empty beer glass inside.

Theresa giggled at his dramatic gesture, prompting Helen to elbow her in the ribs.

"Mr. McGarry, why did ye come back to the weddin' after Bridie told ye to go home?" Anna asked, unamused by Neil's behavior.

He took a wobbly step toward Anna. "I heard from Bridie that ye all think I did Saoirse McHugh wrong, and I'm here to tell ye it's all a lie. I'm a good man, and I want to court yer sister."

Anna glared at Bridie. "Ye told him about what I said?"

"Of course, I did. Ye made a judgment about him based on what someone else told ye, someone I don't even know."

"Ye don't trust me? Is that it?"

Bridie backed up a couple feet as Anna drew closer. "I do trust ye, but ye don't trust me."

"Ye're actin' like the child ye are."

"Ye won't let me make mistakes," Bridie said, her voice growing louder. "I can take care of meself just as ye did comin' here."

Anna crossed her arms and looked away. She stayed silent for a moment until she took a deep breath. "I didn't take care of meself when I was alone. I endured a horrific heartbreak I've told none of ye about because I was ashamed. I started courtin' a man who wasn't kind to me. Bridie, I didn't want ye to experience the same. I was, and still am, tryin' to protect ye. To protect all of ye."

"Well, ye have a funny way of showin' it," Neil said, burping at the end.

Bridie frowned at Neil, then turned her attention back to Anna. "I brought Neil and Aunt Nellie to the weddin' because I was angry with all of ye, but especially Anna. I wanted ye to give them a chance and show I can make me own decisions, even if they're the wrong ones. I'm sixteen now, not the same eleven-year-old ye left back in Listowel years ago."

"Ye couldn't have brought them to a family dinner and not to yer sister's weddin'?" Anna asked, cocking her head. "Maybe if ye had introduced us before, they may have been welcomed as guests."

"Well, I—"

"And ye had to go and pick Neil McGarry?"

Bridie shrugged. "He's drunk now, but I believe he's a good man. Ye just have to get to know him. I want ye to know him."

"That sounds splendid to me! But first, I need to meet Miss Mary and give her me present," Neil said, pointing toward the church.

Right on cue, the door opened and out popped Mary. Bridie's stomach dropped. How did she find them? Did she hear Anna raising her voice? Or did she see them bring Neil McGarry outside? Perhaps she had noticed all four of her sisters were missing from her wedding celebration for quite a long time.

"Mary! There's nothin' to see here! We were just comin' back inside," Helen said, rushing toward the door to usher her away.

"I've been listenin' at the door this whole time," Mary said quietly.

Bridie glanced at Anna in a panic.

"I'm not angry. I'm not upset. I'm only sad. I'm sad I have to move in a couple weeks' time, and this is how I'm leavin' ye. We've been fightin', keepin' secrets, lyin' to each other. For what purpose? We have such little time left together."

Bridie looked from Anna to Helen to Theresa. They all stared at the ground in shame. Mary was right.

"I wish something would happen to keep me here," Mary whispered.

And with that, she disappeared back inside the party.

CHAPTER 16

THERESA'S SURPRISE INVITATION

———

Theresa glanced behind her for the third time in a minute. The sun was setting earlier each day, but plenty of light was still out to walk home from the factory without concern. She just couldn't shake the feeling someone was following her. The crowd had thinned considerably over the last few blocks to a pair of older men sharing a newspaper and quarreling about the best stock to purchase. They didn't pay any attention to her quickening pace.

Since the night of the dance at St. Columba's, she'd been much more cautious when walking alone, no matter the time of day. Her petite stature made her feel vulnerable, especially in throngs of people where anyone could push her into an alleyway without causing commotion. The men who approached her outside the dance could've dragged her into the darkness and—

She stopped walking and closed her eyes. If Helen hadn't come looking for her, the men could've done much worse than scare her. They came from the alley, collars popped high enough to reach the brims of their hats. Shadows obscured their faces enough that she couldn't tell them apart, but one man was noticeably taller than the other. The shorter man demanded to know whether she was Theresa Galvin. When she neither confirmed nor denied her identity, the taller man stepped so close to her that her breasts brushed his coat. He smelled of cigars.

Several more times he asked her, but she didn't say a word. He got closer, pushing himself up against her.

"What about your sister, Anna? Did she send you to spy on Mr. Grant?" he whispered; his rancid breath hot in her ear. "You better stay quiet or you'll all pay up. Don't make that mistake."

Theresa didn't know how they knew Anna. She never told Harry her name, and Penny wouldn't have either.

The man looked at his partner, then stepped back. "You must see Mr. Grant when he calls you."

Those were the only instructions she had received before Helen ran toward them and scared the men back into the alley. She could barely remember what they looked like several weeks later, but she was certain she hadn't seen them again. Penny Grant had become a stranger, too. Every night Theresa normally helped out, she called Penny and told her she either felt under the weather or needed to take care of important matters at home. By the fifth call, she was sure Penny would let her go, but each time she wished Theresa the best and that she hoped to see her soon. How could she and Harry be married? Was Penny in on whatever was going on?

The men sharing the newspaper passed on Theresa's left. She opened her eyes and watched them each repeatedly point to different parts of the wrinkled pages. Now, she followed them. Up ahead on her right, the park where she first met

Penny came into view. It was much more deserted, only a few children throwing around a baseball and a lone couple sitting on a bench. The grass had grown a straw yellow, courtesy of this year's early frost according to the *Farmers' Almanac.* A strong wind had undressed most of the trees in the first week of October, much too early in the season. She hadn't taken this route home in a long time.

With the men far ahead of her, Theresa glanced behind her to see if she was completely alone. In the distance, a figure carrying what looked like a box was running toward her. She squinted. Her vision wasn't any less blurry. It looked like a woman. She was holding a hatbox with a ribbon tied around it. Where was she going in such a hurry? The woman started waving at her.

"Theresa! Is that you?" she hollered.

It was none other than Penny Grant. Theresa stood there, her mouth slightly open. They weren't supposed to cross paths. She had made that request in her bedtime prayers every day this week. The Lord had never turned a deaf ear to her before.

Penny slowed down to walk, her breaths heavy between embarrassed laughs. "Did you not recognize me back there calling your name?"

"I thought it was ye, but I just wanted to be sure!" Her voice was too cheerful.

"I inherited my mother's terrible eyesight, so I imagine I would've done the same," Penny said, putting the box on the ground.

Theresa tucked a curl behind her ear. "So where are ye comin' from?"

"I was running a few errands while the kids are at the neighbor's. Without your help these past weeks, I've found myself growing impatient with the children. Just picking up a mended hat has helped clear my mind and made me realize how much I need you back."

Theresa looked at her feet. "I-I would love to come help ye again, but I'm afraid—"

"Is it something I've done? Am I gone for too long talking to neighbors when you're watching the children?" Penny's voice was higher than a kettle whistle.

Theresa shook her head too vigorously. "It's not ye at all, Penny. I have other responsibilities that have fallen on me at home. Ye and the children are absolutely wonderful."

Penny smiled, her whole body visibly relaxing. "Thank goodness! I thought I had scared you away somehow. Of course, I'm disappointed you won't be able to come back and work for me, but I'm glad it was for another reason, whatever your responsibilities may be."

Theresa didn't know what else to say. She and Penny were friendly, but for the most part, she stayed out of the house when Theresa looked after the children. They didn't have much in common other than witnessing the physical demonstration of a certain man's private desires, unwillingly on Theresa's part. She looked from the hatbox up to Penny's face, hoping she'd have to suddenly drop it off somewhere in a hurry.

Penny followed Theresa's obvious glance but didn't pick up the hatbox. Instead, she clasped her hands behind her back and divulged a simple fact that made Theresa weak in the knees for the wrong reason.

"I told Harry about hiring you."

Theresa just stared at her for a moment, then cleared her throat. "Ye what?"

"I believed he ought to know why I've been feeling quite taxed lately. He loved the idea of bringing in help and requested you join us for dinner one evening. Of course, that is whenever it suits you best."

"Harry wants to meet me...for the first time?"

Penny tilted her head. "Have you two met before?"

Theresa realized her mistake. "Silly me, I meant that he wants to meet me for the first time after I've quit the job?"

"Please come, Theresa. He wants to give his thanks for helping me when I felt no one else could."

When Harry called her, she had to meet him. The men made that clear. He had cornered her once again. Taking a deep breath, Theresa nodded with a tight-lipped smile.

Penny picked up the hatbox. "I knew you'd agree! He's going to be overjoyed when I tell him."

"I'm sure that excitement will carry through yer night together," Theresa said under her breath.

"What was that?" Penny asked.

"I said I hope that excitement will carry the night we have dinner together."

"I'm positively delighted just thinking about it now. Please call when you figure out what night will work!" Penny waved, then crossed the street.

"I certainly will!" Theresa called after her.

She certainly had to.

CHAPTER 17

MARY GOES
TO THE BANK

———

Going to the bank was the last errand on Mary's Wednesday to-do list. She needed to deposit her second-to-last paycheck before moving to Pittsburgh in a few weeks. Since she finished her necessary duties before lunch, Mary was granted a half day as a reward for her productivity and took the opportunity to run some errands. After picking up a dress from the tailors and dropping off some flowers to old Mrs. Brandy for her birthday, Mary needed to stop by the bank before heading home to help Anna make dinner.

The bank was the only place the wealthy and working class entered for the same reason. Mary loved throwing open the heavy brass door with two hands, the air of propriety and tradition hitting her nose. The white marble floors were spectacularly clean for being so frequently tread upon. Her footsteps always echoed in the high ceilings, reflecting the hush-hush of interactions between tellers and customers. Coming to the bank made her feel important. And this time was no different.

Mary gazed up at the several-story brick building. What did they keep on the floors above the first? Were there piles of money lying around? Stacks of solid gold bars? The dead bodies of bankers past? She'd never gone beyond the lobby, the public's version of the bank, but she secretly longed to explore every nook and cranny of the place. Rich people kept all the secrets of society. And Bridie probably already knew a few of those secrets from O'Hara's.

She opened the door as usual, two-handed with all her strength, and anchored her foot against the bottom to prevent it from swinging right back into her. Taking a deep breath, she stepped into the bank, letting the door close behind her at her slowly. She crinkled her nose. The air was stale, musty as if the windows and doors had been sealed for months. But they hadn't. The bank opened its doors every day at nine o'clock from Monday to Friday.

At first glance, nothing appeared different than any of her other visits. The long red carpet leading to the teller counter hadn't moved. The oil paintings of the bank's previous owners hung in the same order on the left wall. The chandeliers above had the same number of candles. The line was once really long, and she had time to count them. The tellers were dressed in three-piece suits with their hair slicked back with just enough hair oil.

Mary knew Anna had visited the bank on Monday to deposit money from her stock market winnings that hadn't been spent on the wedding. Anna was always quick to notice the smallest of changes in anything, so she probably would've mentioned something, right? Mary shook her head. The unusual late autumn heat must've gotten to her from running all over the city today.

She walked inside the bank a few steps further, then stopped.

There, right at her feet, was a set of dried muddy shoe prints.

It hadn't rained in at least three days. Why hadn't the floors been cleaned since then? Mary looked around the room once more. Balls of dusts were collecting along the walls and in the corners. Cobwebs moved in the chandeliers with any slight wind. The windows were covered in black-and-white bird droppings, and the portraits needed a dedicated feather dusting.

The bank was dirty.

Mary followed the red carpet to the back of the lobby where the teller counter stretched wall to wall. Several people waited in front of her, all of them dressed immaculately. She was still wearing her factory uniform—a simple gray dress with a dingy white apron and black T-strap heels. Those ahead were from the upper class, with their multiple gold rings and perfectly shined Oxfords. But she didn't mind at all. In fact, she enjoyed waiting in the same line. They were equals at the bank. It didn't matter how much were in their respective accounts; they all deposited and withdrew money.

"Excuse me, ma'am," someone behind her said, tapping her right shoulder.

Mary spun around and looked down at a hunched old woman. Dressed in a black fur coat and matching cap, she leaned desperately on her wooden cane. Mary started sweating just looking at her.

"Yes?"

"I saw you looking at the filth. It's a shame how the banks are getting on."

Mary glanced at the muddy footprints, then back at the woman. "Gettin' on?"

"The first sign of failure is dirt. It always has been and always will be."

"Yes…I suppose so." Mary didn't know what the woman was talking about.

"The line is moving, dear," the woman said, pointing with her cane.

Mary turned her attention back to the tellers. The line moved slower than normal. She peeked up ahead and realized only two tellers were open. There were usually six, one at each available window. It was neither a holiday nor an odd time of day. Where were they? Did that many tellers call in sick?

She clasped her hands behind her back. They were sweatier than the first time she'd held hands with Jimmy. The line moved forward. She couldn't hear any conversation between the tellers and customers. They were whispering so low that she could hear footsteps on the floor above. That had never happened before. Blood pumped in her ears like a metronome, a steady monotone beat she couldn't escape.

Her turn came, and she stepped up to the teller. Her feet were anvils.

"Ma'am?"

"I'm comin'." It didn't sound like her voice.

She rolled back her shoulders and shuffled to the counter on the left. She could barely see above it. The tellers sat high up, looking down at customers like impatient kings listening to the complaints of their subjects.

The entire counter was dusty, except for two rectangular spots where he counted money in front of customers.

"Hello, sir. How are ye doin' today? How's business been goin'?" she asked, reaching into her pocketbook.

The frail gentleman looked up at the ceiling in hesitation. "It has been busy, ma'am. Very busy."

"Busy in a good way, I hope?" Mary chuckled nervously.

"I suppose you could say that ma'am."

"I'm glad, because the muddy footprints have me nervous." She kept her hand on her two weeks' pay.

"Footprints?"

"Yes, the ones by the door." She pointed behind her.

The gentleman nodded. "Oh yes, we're not minding the floors much this week. It's just dirt."

Mary gave a tight-lipped smile. The fur coat woman's words rang in her ear.

"What can I do for you today, ma'am?"

Mary glanced down at the floor. More dust.

"I'd like to withdraw all me money and close me account, sir. Thank ye very much."

CHAPTER 18

HELEN'S REFUSAL

———

Helen couldn't stop thinking about that Bill Rush fella. His handsome smile, how he almost caught her, the way he bowed. Everything seemed so perfect. Even though he lived just down North Bonsall, they still hadn't crossed paths since the night of the dance. Each evening when she walked home from work, she took her time passing by every house, nonchalantly glancing in the windows if the curtains were open. He was quite the mystery man. Their flirtatious conversation had been cut short when Theresa went missing. Going home with her younger sister so shaken wasn't exactly the time to continue that conversation either. All she knew for sure is that he claimed to dance the Walls of Limerick. He hadn't proven it true, though.

On this Wednesday in particular, Helen felt the Lord was going to bless her. She had been to Confession almost every day in the last two weeks and done her best to keep her nose in her own business. Of course, she accidentally read a page or two of Bridie's diary, but only because it had been sitting open on her bureau. Other than that, she had been well-behaved compared to her past actions. And good behavior deserved to be rewarded.

She turned onto North Bonsall as usual. Multicolored rowhouses lined both sides of the street. Most were constructed with traditional red brick, but no two were exactly the same, much like the Galvin sisters themselves. Awnings, window trims, and door styles set the otherwise identical homes apart. Passing each one, she judged the owner's taste in design as if she were sitting in the last pew at Mass looking at all the hats that shouldn't have been worn. The first house on her right added window boxes full of chrysanthemums. Helen nodded in approval. The second house's front door needed a new coat of red paint. The winter would take care of stripping what was left.

While moving onto the third house, she noticed out of the corner of her eye the paint-chipped door open. An orange cat escaped and leapt down the stairs, then scurried past her up the street.

"Dammit! I thought I locked up that Houdini securely enough."

Helen looked away from the disappearing cat to the Bill Rush standing with two fists on his hips. The Lord really knew how to bless a devout, single woman.

"I'm sure he'll return after he's caught a mouse," Helen said, waving with her fingers.

Bill grinned wide enough to show every last crooked tooth. "Miss Helen Galvin! What a wonder it is to see you again."

"I've been askin' meself when we were goin' to run into each other."

He walked to the bottom step and leaned over the iron railing. "It must be my lucky day then. How have you and Theresa been faring since the dance?"

"We've been just fine. Theresa's still bein' quiet, but nobody's bothered us. She stopped visitin' an older woman from the parish she was takin' care of after work. Mary had her weddin' a few weeks back."

Bill lifted an eyebrow. "And I wasn't your guest of honor?"

"Well, I would've…I should've…I see that—" she stammered, shifting her gaze from his smirk to the chipped red paint on the door.

He jumped off the stair and closed some distance between them. "Wanamaker's should start selling rouge in the color of your natural blush. It's much more becoming than you must feel."

Helen turned her face away, trying to hide her laughter. "I was tryin' to say that Bridie brought two uninvited and disliked guests, so me bringin' another would've been a fiasco."

Bill gasped theatrically and placed both hands over his heart. "Am I that disliked in the Galvin household?"

"Jesus, Mary, and Joseph, I can't seem to say anythin' right in front of ye!" Helen covered her face with her hands and peeked through her fingers at him.

"That's quite alright, Miss Helen. At the next shindig, we'll have to let the dancing speak for you."

She spread her fingers wider, revealing a small smile, then crossed her arms over her chest. "I can promise ye're not disliked in the household. Ye're just not known."

"That's a mighty shame, don't you think? We should change that."

"I think the only way to change that is to have ye over for dinner one night."

Bill looked her up and down, seeming to consider the sincerity of her offer. Shifting his weight from one foot to the other, he stroked his chin for a moment and narrowed his eyes.

An accidental giggle escaped her lips. He broke out into a huge smile and clapped his hands once.

"Just tell me when and where, and I'll be there early with hands full."

"Ye'll already be on Anna's good side without even sayin' anythin'."

Bill winked. "As my aunt says, the less I talk, the better. I don't want to keep you from returning home at a decent hour, so just come knocking when you've got my dinner invitation."

"I'll be sure to come by soon," Helen said, turning away.

"It was a pleasure seeing you again, Miss Helen. Have a wonderful evening."

Helen looked over her shoulder and waved. "I certainly will now that I've seen ye again."

Surprised at her forward flirtation, she watched him wave back but didn't want her gaze to linger too long. Mira Jameson said to leave a man wanting more, a woman should give less of herself, or at least that's what she learned from flirting with every man outside O'Hara's. Helen had never been liked much by the boys growing up. In America, she rarely approached men and instead let them come to her or had one of her sisters introduce them. It was easier than being turned down for another beautiful gal.

Helen started down the street once again, but she didn't critique the rowhouses. Her mind drifted to an imaginary dinner with Bill and her sisters. Theresa already liked him for being a gentleman and walking them home after the dance. But would the others? She didn't even know if he was Irish. That wouldn't matter to her. He danced the Walls of Limerick, but the dance wasn't difficult to learn. What if he was English? Her family would most certainly disown her then. It was one thing for their older brother Mickey to marry an

English woman, but for her to get involved with an English man, even if he was American born....

She shook her head. Anna had been completely wrong about Jimmy Higgins being a Protestant. Helen couldn't travel the same dangerous road. Bill was a kind man interested in her, and she was more than interested in him. That's all she knew. There was no use speculating and getting her knickers in a twist.

Her house came into view. Compared to Bill's, the Galvin residence was straight out of a Sears catalog. The window-panes were newly painted blue, thanks to Jimmy. He also scrubbed the windows after hearing Bridie complain she couldn't see her own reflection. The stairs leading up to the front door were free of any dirt. Anna made a habit of sweeping them before and after work. They all prided themselves in keeping a tidy home, mostly for themselves but also partly for their reputation.

When Helen reached the stairs, she unlaced her leather boots and yanked them off. The stairs were somewhat clean, so she didn't want to add to the filth if Anna had already swept. Picking up both boots with one hand, she marched up the steps and noticed the door was slightly open. Mary had left the factory early to run some errands. She must've been home already. Helen pushed the door open more to find Mary frantically pacing back and forth in the sitting room.

"What's happened?" she asked, dropping her boots.

Mary jumped at her question and placed a palm on her forehead. "I didn't hear ye come in."

Helen chuckled. "The little shriek gave it away."

Mary relaxed her shoulders but began tapping her foot in place.

"Ye're more nervous than when Bridie almost missed the weddin'. What's wrong?"

"We need to take all of our money out of the bank today."

Helen squinted. "What?"

"We need to take every last penny any of us has made out of the bank today."

"Why?"

Mary looked at the ceiling. "Somethin' is wrong with the bank, Helen. Very, very wrong."

"Didn't Anna just go on Monday? She would've certainly said somethin' then."

"I know, but I stepped foot in the bank today and somethin' was wrong. I could feel it in me bones."

Helen closed the door, then turned back to her jittery sister. "What was wrong?"

"Everythin', and I mean absolutely everythin', was dirty."

Helen just looked at Mary, unsure of how to respond. Sometimes she wasn't sure whether the gypsy had given her another strange idea.

"The floor hadn't been mopped. The portraits were dusty. The chandeliers had cobwebs. It's never been that filthy."

"I'm not certain if Anna's been gettin' to yer head with all the cleanin' or—"

"There's somethin' wrong with the bank. Somethin's goin' to happen if we don't withdraw all of our money today."

Helen walked over to one of their faded armchairs and sat down. "Have ye already taken out yer own money?"

Mary nodded. "And we must take out the rest."

"I'm not understandin' how the floor bein' dirty has to do with our money bein' safe," Helen said, smoothing the back of her hair.

"Have ye not been readin' the papers? The market has been stormier than me trip over the Atlantic. If the bank wasn't in trouble, they'd be focusin' on keepin' it clean."

"The market is fine. I saw a dip today, but we have nothin' to be concerned about. It's happened before."

Mary crossed her arms and began pacing again. "The bank closes in an hour. We need to go to get the remainin' money out."

"It's goin' to be fine. When Anna gets home, she'll agree with me."

"What will I agree with?" Anna asked, walking in at just the right moment.

"Miss Mary here is tellin' me we must take all of our money out of the bank today because the floor's dirty."

Anna laid her pocketbook on the foyer table. "There's no need. I was just there on Monday and everythin' was fine."

"I guess the matter is settled," Helen said, glancing from Anna to Mary.

"When somethin' happens, ye'll know I warned ye. Ye'll know I was right all along. I'm spendin' the night at Jimmy's, so don't come after me." Mary threw her pocketbook over her shoulder and rushed past Anna in the doorway, avoiding Helen altogether.

When the door slammed shut, Anna walked into the sitting room and lowered herself into the armchair opposite Helen.

"Do ye think she's worried about the move?" she asked.

Helen contemplated the possibility. Mary hadn't mentioned Pittsburgh since the night Jimmy came to dinner to celebrate the engagement, which was more than a month ago. They were due to move within two weeks. Helen knew Mary hadn't started packing yet. She wasn't usually one to lose her head so easily, but the bizarre outburst indicated otherwise.

"I suppose. Do ye think she's with child? I can't remember the last time she was this set on somethin'."

Anna clasped her hands in her lap. "I was wonderin' that meself, but I'm unsure. All I know is that everythin' will be fine."

Helen nodded. "Yes, just fine."

CHAPTER 19

THE STOCK
MARKET CRASH

———

"Come quickly! They're telling us what's happened!"

Anna wrapped her shawl around her shoulders and grabbed her lunch tin from the bench in the break room. It was the end of a long Thursday, and she was ready to go home. Quite a raucous was coming from the far end of the floor near the stairs. The women who hadn't left yet flocked to the radio Harry Grant used to listen to the news at noon every day.

For the last several hours, men had been yelling in the street, but no one could hear them clearly over the whirring of the sewing machines. The newsboys had passed by, too, shouting something about stock dropping fast. Anna didn't think much of it. The market had been rising and dropping the last several weeks without issue. The experts quoted in the papers said it always corrected itself, and she trusted the experts. Mary trusted the cleanliness of the bank.

Walking toward the small crowd, she glanced outside. The sidewalks were packed with men holding their hats to their heads, rushing off in the direction of something important, she imagined. Newsboys, now pushed onto Fifth Street, stood on their tiptoes waving their papers. Anna made a mental note to buy one. She preferred reading the news in print rather than hearing it from a broadcast. She looked back to the women huddling next to the radio.

"Turn it up!"

Someone fiddled with the volume knob, prompting loud static.

"We need to hear!"

Anna stood at the back of the group. She leaned over to Francis Randall standing next to her. They faced each other at the workstation.

"What is everyone waitin' for?" she asked, looking between the radio and Francis's grim expression.

"Some news on Wall Street. A panic is setting in outside. One of the girls went to buy a paper and couldn't get through the crowd of men."

"In the last hour of trading on Wednesday, October 23—"

"Louder! Louder!"

"—automobile stocks suddenly dropped. Millions of shares were sold in rapid response. This morning of October 24, the opening bell marked a period of selling frenzy after a market loss of 6.3 percent on Wednesday. Prices have since dropped sharply."

The women began murmuring to each other.

"This afternoon, several bankers, headed by Richard Whitney of the New York Stock Exchange, bought a large block of US Steel and encouraged others to step in and support the market. The events on Wall Street are still unfolding as thousands gather outside, wondering about the perceived pandemonium occurring inside the Stock Exchange building at this very moment."

"Do you think the bankers investing so much money will help?" Francis asked.

Anna shrugged. "I suppose so. The men at me parish who advised me own investments said the market couldn't fail. It's been on the rise since I arrived in 1924."

"I just trust the papers to tell my husband what to do."

"Me sister Mary told us to withdraw all our money from the bank yesterday because everythin' was unusually filthy. Do ye suppose the sudden drop has anythin' to do with it?"

Francis shook her head. "At this point in life, I never know what is and what isn't a coincidence."

Anna gazed out the window again at the rushing men. "I think I'm beginnin' to know."

- - -

Even the Monday following the dramatic stock market drop, O'Hara's was as busy as ever. Mondays were always the busiest. Wealthy women preferred a fresh 'do at the start of the week so they wouldn't feel guilty about showing off their most fashionable hats at church on Sundays. Every salon chair was full, including Bridie's. Mira had given her more freedom to handle clients by herself. Her now favorite client, Mrs. Nichols, filled the ten o'clock time slot every Monday morning.

"Make that curl a little tighter, Bridie. My husband has an interview with the *New York* Times today, and I'll be attending at his request."

Bridie nodded, twisting the curler.

The bell above the front door jingled, but she didn't look up. The more experienced stylists liked to greet the customers and inquire about their scheduled appointments.

"The market has dropped again!" a high-pitched voice cried.

Mrs. Nichols twisted her body away from the mirror, causing Bridie to drop a curler. The other stylists and clients looked toward the pair of women clutching each other, a newspaper rolled up underneath one of their arms.

Mira walked toward the women. "I beg your pardon, darlings, but how may we help you here?"

"The market is falling behind, worse than Thursday," they said almost synchronously.

Mira's client stood up from her chair. "What are the papers saying? This must be another selling frenzy, nothing more."

"The papers haven't caught up. I received a phone call from my husband who works as a broker. We're telling all the businesses on the street," the first woman said, unlatching her arms from her friend.

"That can't be true. This is all a hoax," Samantha yelled from the back, waving a comb.

A few clients nodded in agreement, but others exchanged concerned glances.

The woman shook her head. "It's only a matter of time until the news shows up in the papers. Boys will be yelling on every street corner."

"What about my family's money? My husband's shares? His company?" Mira's client asked, her voice rising and dipping like the market.

"My husband said get to the bank before it's too late." The woman grabbed her friend's hand and rushed to the door. "Get to the bank! Tell everyone you know!"

Mrs. Nichols stood up as the bell above the door rang to signal the women's exit. Bridie picked up the curler on the floor before she tripped on it.

"Where are ye goin', Mrs. Nichols?" she asked.

Her older client opened her cream satin pocketbook and rummaged around for a moment. She looked back and forth between Bridie and the front door.

"I must see my husband," Mrs. Nichols said, opening her pocketbook wider.

"Why don't ye let me finish stylin' yer hair first? Ye must look yer best for the interview."

Mrs. Nichols pulled out two crumpled dollar bills and stuffed them into Bridie's hand.

"You're going to need this money much more than me."

Bridie watched her turn around and leave the salon. She had a feeling Mrs. Nichols wouldn't have the interview after all.

- - -

Helen huffed as she ran the final block to their bank. A growing crowd was gathered outside the tall double doors. It was Tuesday at four o'clock. There shouldn't have been a crowd, but every person in Philadelphia with a penny to his or her name felt the same panic, the same desperation she did. The market was plunging like a pilot with a malfunctioning parachute. Everyone could see it, but no one could stop it.

She reached the edge of the crowd out of breath. The bodies were so close together that to penetrate the mob, she'd have to weave like a thread through the eye of a needle. But she didn't care. She needed to get inside the bank. She had already waited long enough, put her own family at risk, convinced them everything would be fine. With the little might she had left, Helen lifted her right elbow and pushed through.

"Watch yourself!" an older man screamed as she shoved by him.

A woman balancing a child on her hip spat on Helen after she almost knocked the child to the ground.

She just kept pushing, elbowing left and right, snaking her way through the horde. She recognized parishioners from St. Columba's, the men who advised Anna on investing in the market. No one saw this coming. No one but Mary.

She saw the front door between the heads of those at the front. They pounded the doors with their fists, red knuckles matching their bloodshot eyes. They were desperate, starved for the promises of their future livelihoods.

The right door opened enough for a person to slide through sideways. People propelled forward like the gates of heaven had been unlocked after being stuck in purgatory. Helen joined the movement. Anna and Theresa and Bridie depended on her. She had ignored Mary's plea, and she must fix her mistake. She had no choice.

A man she didn't recognize stepped out from behind the door, his damp bald head reflecting the afternoon sun. The door closed, and he clasped his hands in front.

"Open the door!" voices yelled in succession.

"We need our money!"

Helen saw the man's lips moving, but all she heard were the crowd's cries. She watched him place his right forefinger and thumb in his mouth and blow. A whistle almost as loud as an incoming train's sounded, and the crowd's jeers settled to a faint murmur.

He cleared his throat. "Ladies and gentlemen, I apologize for the locked doors, but the bank will be closed for the immediate future."

The murmur became agitation.

He took a deep breath and wiped his forehead with a handkerchief. His whole body shook. "No customer may withdraw money until the market recovers considerably. Your money has been invested in the market, but we will make sure to gain every last dollar back. There is no need to panic."

The agitation became fury.

The crowd pushed forward as one, taking Helen with it. She succumbed to the movement, like floating with the current of the River Feale. She looked up to the sky, silencing the ear-piercing screams of those around her who had lost their life savings. The whipped clouds melted together as tears filled her eyes. She saw nothing but light.

O Lord, I ask ye for the strength to tell me sisters we've lost everythin'. I ask ye for the strength to endure their rage. I ask ye for the strength to bear this prideful sin on me soul. For I hold all the blame.

CHAPTER 20

A GREAT LOSS

———

Anna had woken up drenched every morning for the last week. The nightmares kept happening. Satan invaded her dreams every time she experienced a moment of happiness—a plentiful family meal, a dance at St. Columba's, an evening walk home from the factory. He reminded her the money was gone. She would eat only broth and rotten boiled potatoes. She would be too sad to dance with anyone. She would walk home in the evening from the soup kitchen. The Galvin girls would soon be…poor.

She shuddered at the thought. She pushed this grim reality to the back of her mind while walking to the factory with Mary, Helen, and Theresa this morning. Together they had accompanied Bridie to O'Hara's, then strolled in pairs at a slower pace than usual. Since hearing the news, none of them had slept a full night.

Anna glanced at Helen, who mouthed a silent prayer, her lips moving faster than a sewing machine at midday. Helen spent her evenings at church after work going to Confession. She said repenting daily would never make up for ignoring Mary's concerns. She claimed losing the money was all her fault, but Anna felt responsible, too. She had agreed with

Helen's skepticism. Her job was protecting her sisters, yet she failed. And that's why she couldn't face the Lord in his own home. She couldn't admit her failure. She buried it by checking stockings for rips.

The factory appeared ahead, sunbeams extending around its brick walls. Mary's pace quickened. She always entered the building first when the four of them walked together. She loved mingling before the starting bell, but the last several mornings, she kept to herself and only nodded politely when greeted. Anna knew she was worried about money like the rest of them, but she also had Jimmy to think about. No word had come about their move to Pittsburgh. Anna thought about asking once this week. She stopped herself when Mary presented her with the savings she had withdrawn from the bank. Theresa took after Mary, and also tried to give Anna money she had saved in a hatbox. But she refused them both.

They would be fine. They all had jobs. She would protect them this time. The Lord was on her side.

Shadows darkened the factory's exterior to the color of muddy snow. Ivy crawled up the walls and over several of the dirtied windows. Anna wrapped her shawl tighter. Her toes were numb in her boots from the cold.

Mary opened the door and held it for Theresa and Helen. Anna waved her inside and held the door for herself. A sticky warmth enveloped her as she stepped inside the lobby. Women huddled in small groups, jabbering like blackbirds. She couldn't hear one conversation from another, only snippets.

"Did you hear that—"

"—couldn't be true—"

"—cutting that position?"

Anna looked to her sisters who appeared just as overwhelmed as she felt. Theresa latched onto Helen like a newborn onto a mother's breast. Helen wrapped her shawl around Theresa and pulled her closer. Biting her lip, Mary looked at Anna. She only did that when on the verge of crying.

"What do ye think's happenin'?" Mary leaned in and whispered.

"I couldn't tell ye," Anna said.

"The gypsy couldn't either," Mary said to herself.

"Ladies! Ladies!" Mr. Carlton, one of the supervisors, called from the front of the lobby.

Anna stepped closer to Mary and held her hand. The conversations turned to whispers one circle of women at a time.

The obese supervisor licked his thumb and forefinger, then smoothed over the few pieces of hair still on his head. He cleared his throat multiple times, sounding like a motorbike that wouldn't start.

"Ladies, you are to head to your normal positions in a moment. All floor supervisors will be calling you in one by one throughout the day to discuss work changes that are effective immediately."

Whispers filled the room again.

Mr. Carlton cleared his throat once more, the engine starting this time. "Do not converse with each other about the meetings. You shall stay focused on your tasks and complete what must be done before the day's end. Is that clear?"

Anna nodded, looking around at the other women. They didn't seem to have heard him. Their faces were mostly blank, except for squinted eyes and parted lips, like poorly erased chalkboards. She could tell they felt something, but she couldn't read their expressions clearly.

"Alright, that's enough," Mr. Carlton said, clapping his hands. "Off you go to your posts."

The women shuffled toward the stairs at the right side of the lobby. They were a flock of sheep being herded to a familiar pasture, but she didn't know whether they'd just be sheared or killed for meat. Anna worked on the floor above Mary, Helen, and Theresa, so she waved goodbye when they reached their floor. Climbing an additional flight of stairs almost took more physical strength than she could muster. She still couldn't feel her toes.

Opening the door to the fourth floor, Anna expected to see the other women flitting between workstations gossiping, looking out the window, or trying to listen to the radio without Harry Grant hearing. But everything was normal. The women were at their stations focused on their morning tasks. Had she simply imagined the nervous chatter downstairs?

Anna inhaled and walked to her own station. Francis sat across from her. She didn't look up as Anna approached.

"Good mornin', Francis," Anna said, pulling out her stool.

Francis jumped in her seat, then chuckled. "I'm sorry, Anna. I was in a work trance again. Mr. Grant has us all doubling speed this morning."

Anna moved the stool closer to the table and reached for her first pair of stockings to inspect.

"Doublin' speed?"

Francis held a pair of stockings up and stretched the legs gently. "He passed through a few moments ago and told us a big shipment needs to go out tomorrow. Inspection is behind, so we have to double our numbers today."

"I suppose that's doable, but what about gettin' called to his office? Did he say anythin' about that?"

"Nothing at all. I heard from May Mobsby that they're letting a bunch of us go. I suppose if you're called to his office, you're going to be fired."

That's exactly what Anna was afraid of hearing. She placed an elbow up on the table and rested her chin on her hand. The big shipment and double time made sense now. They'd work at full capacity for this last large order and then let workers go. But if business seemed to be booming in spite of the market, why were they firing workers who could fulfill those orders faster? How many would be fired? Would she be fired?

Anna looked down at the stockings lying on the table. No, she wouldn't be fired. The Lord would protect her. She would protect her sisters. It had to be that way.

- - -

The clock struck four. An hour was left before the ending bell and only three women had been called into Harry Grant's office. Anna watched them walk in with fidgeting hands and walk out with sickly complexions. But no tears. They just collected their belongings and left without saying goodbye to anyone. Were they just let go for the rest of the week? Maybe two weeks? The market would get better. It always did. Letting a few workers go was a temporary solution to a temporary problem.

Anna refocused her attention on the last few pairs of stockings she needed to inspect for rips. One pair. Two pairs. Three pairs. Sometimes the repetitive work made her wish she had a job like Bridie's. A job that took more skill than simply making sure her fingernails were filed down to avoid making her own rips when inspecting. Mother was proud all her daughters got good-paying jobs in America, but Anna had wanted something more before the market dropped. She was lucky to have a job at all right now, never mind a more skillful one.

"Miss Galvin!"

She dropped a pair of stockings on her lap. Francis stopped folding the pair in her hands.

"Miss Galvin, please join me in my office for a moment."

Harry Grant wanted to see her. It was her turn to walk in with fidgeting hands and come out with a sickly complexion. But the Lord was on her side. He would take care of her.

The last time Anna passed by his office, she had heard him speaking on the phone about making sure the money had been transferred. She stopped by his door and listened another moment. His belted men needed to be rewarded for their hard work. Anna hadn't the slightest idea what he meant, but it didn't sound aboveboard. Harry Grant caught her walking away when he got off the phone and threatened to fire her unless she minded her own business. From then on, she tried to avoid him at all costs.

She placed the stockings on the table, her hands shaking, and stood up. Francis nodded at her like she was about to face Satan himself. Anna nodded back, then walked to the office. She waited in front of the closed door, afraid to knock. Her time had come. Just as she raised a fist, Harry Grant opened the door and peered down at her with a smirk.

"Thank you for coming, Miss Galvin."

Anna stepped inside his office and he closed the door behind her. She looked at two wooden chairs in front of his desk, but he didn't motion for her to sit. She stood with her back against the wall. He sat in his chair, pulled out a cigar from a drawer, and lit it all while staring at her with the same smirk. Then, he took a drag and let out a puff toward her.

"Miss Galvin, I'm sure you've read all the papers by now. Businesses are already starting to downsize."

She nodded.

Another drag and puff. "And that includes Apex Hosiery, too. We don't have enough clients to offset the number of current workers we have."

Anna swallowed her anger. She wanted to interrogate him about whatever money was transferred to the belted men, but she wouldn't lose her job and her pride in the same day.

"Miss Galvin, I'm afraid I have to let you go. Your hard work will be missed. You may gather your things and leave before the ending bell. Your final pay will be ready for pickup next Friday."

Anna studied Harry Grant's smirk. He wasn't sorry at all, taking drag after drag of that cigar. She wanted to slap him across the face. But she restrained herself and gave him a sad smile. Today she would commit no sins.

"Mr. Grant, it has been a pleasure workin' for ye. May I inquire about me sisters? Will their jobs be safe?"

He put out the cigar in a crystal dish on his desk. "I don't know, Miss Galvin. I don't supervise them, but I can assure you Miss Theresa Galvin will be in good hands. You don't need to worry."

Anna tilted her head. Why did he mention Theresa specifically? As far as she knew, the two had never met. She also warned all of them to stay away from Harry Grant.

"Miss Galvin, please be on your way now. I have much to accomplish before heading home."

"Of course, sir. Have a lovely evenin'."

She showed herself out and headed back to her workstation. She grabbed her belongings and walked around the table to hug Francis, who was still folding stockings and placing them into boxes.

"Keep yer head down and stay out of trouble. The Lord will watch over ye," she whispered into Francis's ear.

Francis nodded, her eyes glassy. Anna winked and wrapped her shawl around her shoulders. A half hour remained before the evening bell, so no one else was headed for the stairs. She walked alongside the wall facing the street. Anna peered out the window to see her three younger sisters stepping onto the sidewalk, belongings in hand and heads down.

They had beat her to it.

CHAPTER 21

DINNER AT THE GRANTS'

———

Six o'clock had almost arrived, and Theresa's stomach whimpered. She wasn't hungry, though. In fact, she hadn't been hungry all day. The only thing she could think about was the dinner at Harry Grant's that night. She had to face him again (this time hopefully clothed) but couldn't find the courage to get herself ready and presentable. Theresa had no idea what he wanted with her. The Lord didn't seem to have any answers either.

Only three days ago, she, Helen, and Mary had lost their jobs cutting stocking fabric. Their floor supervisor, Mr. Henry, had called them into his office together, just as they had expected. Only when Mr. Henry ushered them out, he pulled her to the back and handed her a folded piece of paper. Theresa held it in her fist until she walked into her bedroom an hour later. The crumpled note was on official company letterhead.

Miss Theresa Galvin,

I know who you are. Please join Penny and I for dinner at six thirty sharp on Friday evening. Do not tell your sisters. Come alone.

Harry Grant

Theresa had read the note a half dozen times, then stuck it in her pocketbook. She hadn't looked at it since. Should she burn it before leaving? On second thought, it was probably unnecessary. Anna and Helen were too preoccupied scouring the job advertisement sections of every newspaper available in Philadelphia. Mary spent her time packing and unpacking her clothing for Pittsburgh, and Bridie still had her job in spite of the few client appointments. While saying grace before supper last night, Anna begged the good Lord to let Bridie keep her job until at least she found her own. Theresa was sure a tear dripped into Anna's potatoes as she bowed her head.

She hoped they didn't miss her at supper tonight. Anna had been cooking rather extravagant meals for weekdays and without a steady means of making money. The last judgment seemed to be coming soon, and they couldn't eat earthly food in heaven. That is if they all went to heaven. Bridie had some repenting to do before the Lord came.

Theresa decided to hide Harry Grant's note in between folded bloomers in her undergarment drawer. No one would go looking there. She closed the drawer and gazed at herself in the hand mirror lying on the bureau. It was a terribly unflattering angle. Her cheeks were too pale. A dash of rouge and a few pinches would suffice. She didn't want Penny noticing how unwell she felt.

After fixing her appearance, Theresa nodded at her reflection and walked downstairs toward the kitchen. She peeked inside the doorway to find Anna rolling out some bread dough.

"What are ye makin'?" she asked.

Anna jumped at Theresa's voice. "Ye're goin' to send me to the grave before the Lord's ready to take me."

Theresa bit her lip. Her light tread was a blessing and a curse.

Anna stopped rolling the dough and squinted. "Why do ye have so much color on yer cheeks?"

"I'm goin' to a friend's house for dinner tonight. I just came in to tell ye."

"But I was goin' to make yer favorite before all of the good food went to waste!"

Theresa looked at her shoes. An extra Hail Mary would be in order. "I can't miss this dinner because me friend may have a job opportunity for me."

Anna's face lit up like Wanamaker's grand window display at Christmas. Her expression dimmed just as quickly.

"Does this friend of yers work at the factory?"

Theresa pressed her palms together behind her. "No…it's a friend I met…at the park."

It wasn't technically a lie. She did meet Penny at the park. Maybe tonight would only require a Hail Mary and a half.

"Well, tell yer friend I said hello and thank her for thinkin' of ye for that job," Anna said, turning back to the dough.

It would probably be best if she did neither.

- - -

Standing outside the Grant family home was like peering into a past life. Only a month had passed since the incident, but it felt so much longer. Theresa buried her nose into her knitted scarf and hugged herself tighter beneath her wool shawl. The wind had picked up on her walk over. The Grants had a healthy fire going and the smoke rising from their chimney drifted in her direction. She wanted to float along with it.

As she gazed at the smoke plume, the front door opened with a soft creak. Penny stood there beaming, a baby in each arm like when Theresa had seen her the first time in the park.

"Theresa! It's absolutely wonderful to see you," Penny said, leaning in for an armless embrace. The babies dipped forward with her movement, their eyes wide with confusion.

The hummingbird flutter in her stomach slowed to a goose flap. George and Maggie had gained neck control since she last saw them. Theresa didn't realize how much she'd missed them. Wrapping her arms awkwardly around Penny and the twins, she felt at ease and momentarily forgot that Penny was married to Harry.

Penny pulled back when Maggie fussed. "Dinner is already steaming on the table, so no need to wait to dig in! Let's get you inside and seated. I just have to put the babies in their cradles and convince Michael to read a book in his bed."

"Do ye need any help with the children?" Theresa asked out of habit.

Penny shook her head and winked. "No, you need not worry about me. I've become much better at getting them to sleep since you left."

Theresa let out a quiet giggle. Her quitting did some good for both of them.

"What I can ask you to do is sit down at the table and start helping yourself to some food," Penny said, stepping aside to let Theresa inside the house.

"I suppose I'm startin' to get hungry about now."

Theresa followed her through several sitting rooms that looked the same into a dining room twice the size of the Galvin sisters'. She had never seen this part of the house while employed. The children's bedrooms and kitchen were where she stayed put.

The table, which sat sixteen people, was completely covered in dishes. Roast beef, candied yams, asparagus, biscuits, apple pie—a real holiday feast in October. It reminded her of when Anna and Mary decided to cook supper together after they stopped arguing. The only difference was the Grants could afford to spend more lavishly than the dozens of people fired from the factory.

Penny pulled the nearest chair out with her foot. "Theresa, please take a seat and start filling your plate. We have more than enough to feed the neighborhood."

"I certainly won't pass up yer hospitality."

"I'll be back in a few moments!" Penny called as she walked back through the sitting rooms toward the stairs, bouncing the babies with each step.

Theresa didn't know what to fill her plate with. She wanted a bite of everything. When would she get to eat the butcher's most expensive cut of meat? Certainly not in her household this year. They would soon be eating boiled potatoes and broth for every meal. She wouldn't mind, but Bridie would be sick of it after one day. Theresa chuckled to herself as she reached over to spoon some sliced carrots onto her plate.

"Miss Theresa Galvin, I'm so glad you could join Penny and I for dinner this evening," Harry Grant said, strolling in from the kitchen with a bottle of red wine in hand.

Theresa nearly dropped the serving spoon onto her plate. She was so focused on Penny and the children that she forgot the reason she came at all—the note hidden in her bloomers drawer at home.

Harry Grant pulled out the chair right across from Theresa and sat down. He made a show of unfolding the linen cloth and placing it on his lap. Then, he reached for the wine bottle to his left and pulled out the cork with little effort. After pouring himself a rather full glass, he looked at Theresa's empty one and gestured with the bottle.

"No thank ye, sir. I don't drink."

He placed the bottle back on the table and folded his hands in front of his empty plate. They sat in silence until Theresa's stomach rumbled audibly.

"I'm sorry to hear all your sisters lost their jobs."

Theresa nodded, keeping her eyes on the carrots. "I'm hopeful they'll find work soon. Philadelphia's a large city."

"I doubt it. The city's job market is shrinking by the hour."

She said nothing.

"You won't need to worry about your job because I have a proposal for you. All you need to do is retrieve one thing for me and you can have your job back."

Theresa looked up from the carrots. Harry Grant's smirk made the hairs on her arms stand up.

"Bring me the emerald necklace."

Bridie's...emerald necklace? The one some men tried to steal? The one that led to Bridie's fall? Theresa fought the urge to stand up and yell for Penny.

"How—how do ye know about it?"

Harry Grant took a sip of his wine, then smiled. His teeth were already stained light purple.

"I have eyes everywhere, Miss Theresa." He lowered his voice. "With the recent plunge in the market, I have a very important person to pay back. That necklace is worth more than you or your sisters realize."

She grabbed the sides of her chair.

"I'll even raise the stakes of the deal. In addition to giving you your job at the factory back, I'm offering you a temporary raise the next several months in addition to the privilege of watching the children. That should be more than enough to supplement the money your sisters won't be making. But in return, I need the necklace and your silence."

Theresa stood up, pushing the chair back. She looked from the carrots to Harry Grant. Did she hear him correctly? He wanted her to steal from her own sister?

"The offer is good for twenty-four hours. If you agree and bring me the necklace, you can have your jobs back by the end of the week."

She didn't know what to say to this man. All she knew was she needed to leave. Anna's face flashed in her mind.

"Thank ye for dinner, sir. I must go home now."

Theresa wrapped her shawl around her shoulders and ran out the front door without saying goodbye to Penny.

CHAPTER 22

THERESA CONFIDES
IN HER SISTERS

———

Theresa burst into the dining room the moment Anna finished saying grace. Her sisters still had their heads bowed and eyes closed. Bridie was the first to look up and see Theresa bent over, trying to catch her breath.

"Was a rabid dog chasin' ye home or somethin'?" Bridie asked, pushing the water pitcher closer to Theresa.

The others glanced up in surprise. She knew they were expecting her to be gone for another few hours.

Helen grabbed the pitcher and poured Theresa a glass. "Why are ye home so early? Did the dinner fall through?"

"Did ye get the job?" Anna snatched the glass away before Helen finished pouring and handed it to Theresa.

She glanced at the glass in her hand but didn't take a sip. Her tongue felt stiff like a piece of wet clothing left to dry overnight in January. This was the first time she'd speak about the situation aloud. Her consistent lies would be exposed. Would the Lord cast her down right there in the dining room? She had hidden the truth from her sisters for their protection…for her own. It would be best to confide in Anna first and save herself the shocked gasps and subsequent reprimands from the others. Her early presence already created an unnecessary stir.

"Anna, I need to speak with ye privately."

"Why would ye need to talk to Anna?" Helen asked.

Mary nodded. "We're all worried sick sittin' here lookin' at ye."

"Was I right about the rabid dog?" Bridie raised her eyebrows.

Theresa regretted even saying she needed to talk to Anna. She should've just pulled her into the other room. Of course, the others would likely eavesdrop and barge into the conversation anyway. They were sisters after all. Sometimes she forgot.

"Whatever it is, ye can tell all of us," Anna said, raising her chin.

She inhaled deeply and looked from one sister to another around the table. She couldn't imagine what they expected her to say. Nothing possibly more absurd than what she was about to divulge. That is unless they thought she was pregnant.

"Harry Grant wants me to give him Bridie's emerald necklace in exchange for gettin' me job back."

Her sisters didn't react. They just stared at her, eyes narrowed and lips pursed.

Anna cleared her throat. "Harry Grant, me former supervisor?"

"Yes, Harry Grant the supervisor."

"How does he know ye? Nobody's met him but Anna," Mary said, resting her chin on her hand.

"I started helpin' his wife put their children to bed durin' the week."

Helen shook her head. "I knew ye were too pleasant comin' home those nights for lookin' after an old woman."

"How in the world did ye meet his wife?" Anna asked.

"Well…I was on me way home from work and escorted a little boy back to his mother in the park."

Helen nodded slowly. "Did ye know that mother was Harry Grant's wife?"

"Not at first, but when she offered me the job I did."

"Theresa Galvin, I will drag ye to Confession tomorrow for tellin' enough lies to fill a Bible, but I need to understand why he's desirin' the necklace," Anna said.

Theresa rocked back and forth on her heels. They didn't need to know how she and Harry Grant met exactly. Going to Confession for the next year was tolerable. Ending up in a convent would be punishment.

"The short story is Harry Grant found out I was a Galvin girl. He's somehow involved with that gang that tried to rob the necklace from Bridie—"

"How did they know it was us?" Bridie asked.

Theresa sighed. "I don't know how they figured it out. All I know is he needs the necklace to pay back someone he owes money—money he doesn't have."

Anna pushed her chair away from the table and stood up. "That lowlife scoundrel! I warned ye not to get involved!"

"Those men at the dance…" Helen said to herself.

"Yes, Harry Grant sent those men."

"That son of a—"

"Mary Galvin! The Lord is listenin' even in times of anger," Anna said, hands on her temples.

Bridie sniffled. "Ye better not be givin' him me necklace!"

Anna placed her hands flat on the table and leaned forward. "She will absolutely not be givin' him anythin'. Not her word, not her labor, not the necklace."

Theresa wanted to sit on the floor and pull her knees to her chest. How had she gotten herself into this mess? Why hadn't she told her sisters the moment she felt endangered? Why had she taken the job with Penny in the first place knowing her husband was Harry Grant?

"Did he threaten ye if ye didn't hand over the necklace?" Anna asked.

"No, he didn't. But if I did give him the necklace, he'd give me a raise and pay me to watch the children, too."

Helen stood up and walked over to Theresa, placing a hand on her shoulder. "No amount of money is worth givin' that man what he wants."

"Not even when I've lost me job today?"

Everyone turned to look at Bridie, who had tears running down her face.

Helen took her hand off Theresa's shoulder. "Ye what?"

"I was let go today. I didn't want to tell ye because I was yer last hope," Bridie cried.

Mary leaned over and wiped away Bridie's tears. "Ye weren't the last hope because we still have hope. We'll always have hope."

"I check the job ads in the papers every day because I have hope. Helen goes to the bank every day to check for our money because she has hope," Anna said.

Theresa's eyes watered. "I won't give Harry Grant the necklace because I have hope."

"Jimmy and I have hope, too. And so we're not movin' to Pittsburgh until I know ye're all back on yer feet."

Bridie jumped up and hugged Mary, almost knocking her off the chair. Anna clasped her hands together and looked up at the ceiling. Helen threw her hands in the air and spun in a circle. For the first time since Bridie arrived, Theresa felt utter joy in the room with her four sisters. There were no lies, no secrets, no gossip between them. There were no arguments, no accusations, no lectures.

They were just happy.

And hopeful.

CHAPTER 23

HELEN SEEKS HELP

———

Helen couldn't look at another newspaper without feeling hopeless. Two weeks had passed, and nothing was in any of the local job advertisement sections. In fact, the "Help Wanted" ads were being quickly replaced with "Looking to Help" ads. The number seemed to double by the day. To distract herself from the papers, Helen continued to visit the bank out of habit, but she knew deep down they'd never get their savings back.

Anna and Mary started fixing holes in and hemming clothing for fellow parishioners and Bonsall Street neighbors for a small fee. They used the scrap fabric Mary had collected over the years. The few cents they made with each return added up and helped with rationing the little money they had left. Bridie also started giving haircuts and styling updos for those who couldn't afford to go to O'Hara's any longer. And Theresa took up indoor gardening in November to grow vegetables and herbs. Anna even said a dozen prayers a day to St. Fiacre, but she was sure even those daily dozen prayers wouldn't make the seeds grow in pewter bowls.

After Theresa didn't bring the emerald necklace to Harry Grant, Anna and Helen hadn't been letting her out of their sight. They spent most time at home and at St. Columba's and occasionally went to the grocer's. Whenever she went somewhere, one of them went with her. Helen sensed Theresa was starting to grow tired of their company, but she never complained. She knew better.

Just like walking Theresa everywhere wouldn't last long, their efforts of sewing, styling, and gardening wouldn't either. They needed reliable jobs with weekly payments. Even with Jimmy chipping in some of his salary to help pay rent and food, they would probably run out by the new year. Helen also felt guilty that Jimmy paid anything at all. He was family now, but he wasn't a Galvin. Mary had become a Higgins. They needed help from a Galvin.

Neither she nor her sisters would ever dare ask Mother or Father for any financial help. They were already burdened enough with farming expenses and the rest of the siblings to feed. Helen wasn't even sure if they knew about the market crash. News from America traveled slowly to Listowel without being shared directly in a letter. She guessed Anna had left out the many events from the past month in her letters. Otherwise, Mother would sell every last piece of clothing she had to send money over.

Then, Helen thought of Aunt Nellie. They hadn't seen or heard from her since Mary's wedding. Now looking back, they had reacted pretty harshly to her coming. She was just family they had never met. In a way, she was the closest thing they had to home besides each other.

Now sitting on her bed with a spread of newspapers in front of her, Helen felt a pang of homesickness stronger than City Hall's clock striking one. She longed for the familiar, even if it wasn't familiar to her just yet. She needed to visit Aunt Nellie not only for her own sake but also for her sisters' livelihoods. Anna would certainly disapprove, but she didn't have a choice. Family relied on family. And Aunt Nellie was family.

- - -

Mornings in mid-November were much colder than Helen remembered. Then again, she had never really gotten used to the extreme weather conditions in the northeast. It grew cold and rained often in Listowel, but the summers weren't blistering, and the winters didn't turn her feet to the ice blocks Jimmy sold for a living.

Approaching Aunt Nellie's house, Helen wondered if her sisters really believed she was running errands. She didn't know Aunt Nellie's address, so she had to ask Bridie under the guise of collecting addresses early for Christmas greeting cards. It worked. And now here she was, walking up the same path her youngest sister had followed several weeks before. The spherical holly bushes were, in fact, as perfect as Bridie had described. Who trimmed them? The property's landscaping was immaculate.

Helen shuffled up the walk, looking at each holly bush. Still not a single one overgrown. She gazed up at the three-story stone home. Aunt Nellie lived all by herself. Bridie had described the magnificence and stateliness of the home, but Helen only saw the loneliness. How could a single older woman take care of everything? Where was her family? Then, she remembered the sisters were her family. Aunt Nellie was a childless widow.

Continuing to the porch, Helen tiptoed up the stairs to avoid squeaking floorboards. Aunt Nellie could be sitting next to a nearby window or standing behind the front door for all she knew. But she was here to visit Aunt Nellie, wasn't she? Helen had come to see her, not hide from her. Taking a deep breath in, Helen marched forward and knocked on the door three times, a little harder than she had intended.

Less than a moment later, Aunt Nellie cracked the door and poked her head out. Her faded red hair hung over her shoulder in a braid. Her expression changed instantly from suspicion to warm surprise, pursed lips stretching into a toothy grin. She threw open the door and extended her arms for a hug without even saying a word.

Helen just stood there, a half-smile on her face. She didn't know whether to return the hug or try a handshake. She'd never had a real conversation with Aunt Nellie before. They were strangers related by blood and spirit. Yet somehow, she felt drawn to reciprocate the hug.

Helen must've waited too long because Aunt Nellie stepped forward and pulled her in. She placed a hand behind Helen's head and the other between her shoulder blades. The embrace felt so foreign. Helen hadn't realized how little she hugged her sisters. They squeezed each other's shoulders and linked arms, but hugs were few and far between. Her body craved a more caring touch.

"Dear, will ye please join me inside?" Aunt Nellie whispered, giving her a tight squeeze.

Despite the teeth-chattering wind, Helen strangely didn't want to go inside. When walking over, she had every intention of sitting with Aunt Nellie in her secret garden parlor as Bridie had described. But now, something felt different. She only deserved to go inside when money wasn't on her mind.

Helen untangled herself from Aunt Nellie's tight grip and stepped back toward the stairs. "I think I'll just go. Comin' here was a mistake. I apologize for wastin' yer time."

"Dear, please come inside. I'm afraid ye'll catch pneumonia before ye return home."

"No, I must get home," Helen said, turning toward the yard.

Aunt Nellie stepped out of the doorframe and closed the door behind her. "Why did ye come all this way just to leave after sayin' hello?"

Helen looked behind her shoulder at her aunt standing there shivering. She couldn't find the words, so her body found them for her. The first tear was warm on her cheek. The rest burned like holding frostbitten hands over a fire.

"Oh dear, what's the matter?" Aunt Nellie asked, taking Helen into her arms once more. This time, she let herself relax completely.

Helen wiped away her tears with the back of her mitten. "I'm sorry for me decorum. I don't usually fuss this easily in front of others."

"Hush now, I think about ye and yer sisters every single day. Ye're in me prayers mornin', noon, and night."

"Thank—"

"There's no need to thank me. That's what family does. Now, how have ye all been farin' since I last saw ye?"

Helen pulled back and looked down at the floor. "We've all lost our jobs at the factory and Bridie at O'Hara's. Our money in the bank is gone, too. We're just hopin' to find somethin' that pays a regular wage soon enough."

Aunt Nellie gasped, then covered her mouth. Lowering her hand, she said, "Me dear girls, I'm so terribly sorry that has happened to ye. The Lord will help ye through yer plight. Ye have the support of yer community—yer neighborhood, yer parish. And ye can always count on havin' me unconditional support."

Helen lifted her head. "I'm sorry for the way we treated ye at Mary's weddin'. We should've let ye come and sit with us. Family is family."

"Please don't apologize, dear. I should've known ye'd be harborin' spite. I don't blame any of ye. I believe the Galvin sisters need to stick together. Irish immigrant women need to support each other."

"I think we all realize that now," Helen said, pulling her scarf up over her chin. "How are ye doin' with the crash?"

Aunt Nellie shrugged. "Me life hasn't changed much at all and that makes me feel guiltier than a child committin' a sin right after walkin' out of Confession."

"Why is that?"

"Well dear, me husband didn't believe in banks. He kept every last penny of his money stowed away in different parts of the house. Some ridiculous places, I might add. And I've realized, he's been dead five years, and I haven't touched the money. It's still sittin' there."

Helen said nothing.

"Me dear, what I'm tryin' to say is I want to help ye and yer sisters with whatever ye need. I don't need money to be collectin' dust. I need it to be payin' rent and buyin' food and keepin' ye alive. It's the least I can do for crashin' Mary's weddin' and showin' I want ye to trust me more than anythin'. We're family."

A rogue tear ran down Helen's cheek. She sniffed and rubbed her eyes with mitten-covered fists.

"Thank ye, Aunt Nellie. I'll talk to me sisters. I'm thankful ye're here, and next time I'll come inside."

Her aunt smiled softly, her cheeks rosy like a china doll's. "I'd like that very much, dear."

Helen turned to leave, then thought a moment. "Aunt Nellie?"

"Yes, dear?"

"Would ye like to join us for Thanksgivin'?"

Aunt Nellie's soft smile transformed into the same toothy grin that greeted her when she first opened the door.

"I thought ye'd never ask."

"Ye'll be me special guest. But this time, I promise ye won't be kicked out."

CHAPTER 24

THANKSGIVING TOGETHER

For as much sugar as Anna demanded Helen get from the grocer's, she wasn't sweet about asking. By late morning on Thanksgiving Day, Helen was already exhausted. Anna had ordered everyone up at five o'clock to help with running errands and preparing dinner. She had decided to bake the brown bread later in the day, but when she realized they didn't have enough sugar to even make one batch, Anna almost boiled over like a kettle left on the stove for too long. Helen saved the morning by volunteering to get the sugar just like she had the year before with flour.

It was Helen's third time celebrating Thanksgiving, only this year, more guests would be joining. Of course, there were the five of them plus Jimmy and Aunt Nellie. Bridie had even convinced Anna to let Neil McGarry come for dessert. They were practicing forgiveness in the Galvin house.

Now on the way home from the grocer's, Helen was nearly running down the sidewalk. She hated how frigid November had become. Everyone she passed could see how heavily she was breathing, yet she wasn't warming up one bit. The sack under her arm also weighed more every minute. At least she was almost home. Helen hadn't been paying attention to her surroundings because she wanted to get home before Anna yelled at her.

She turned onto North Bonsall Street and increased her pace. Just another few blocks until she could throw the sugar at Anna. This was like running with an infant, only she was the one whining to herself. Helen hadn't been paying much attention to the houses she passed, like usual, until she saw Bill Rush's.

That sweet man. She had promised him a dinner invitation the last time they spoke. They hadn't crossed paths since that lovely evening before the market crash. Had he lost his job? She realized they had never had a full conversation either. She didn't know him at all, but they didn't live on the same street for nothing.

Helen turned around, walked up the stairs, and knocked on his front door. She felt a strange giddiness in her chest. She wanted to know this Bill Rush, even if it meant they were only friends. He had protected her and Theresa the night of the dance without so much as knowing where they hailed from. He was a decent man, and she didn't have enough decent men in her life.

But Bill Rush didn't seem to be home. It was Thanksgiving after all. He was probably off visiting relatives somewhere in the city. She could call on him another time. Helen walked back down the stairs and hefted the sugar under her other arm.

"Miss Helen Galvin, was that you knocking on my door?"

Helen spun around. Bill Rush stood in his doorway dressed in his Sunday best. He looked exactly the same as she had remembered, beaming smile and all.

The giddiness returned as she scampered to the bottom step and leaned against the handrail.

"I thought ye weren't home, so I was goin' on me merry way!"

"Well, I thought you didn't like me because I never got that dinner invite," Bill said, winking.

Helen shook her head. "I can assure ye I like ye, but we faced a mighty job disaster in the Galvin household. I've been preoccupied with the job ad section of every paper in Philadelphia."

Bill's smile shrank in concern. "I'm so sorry to hear that, Miss Helen. If I hear of anything, I'll be sure to come knocking. I've been lucky so far. No one has been let go yet at my company, but my cat, Houdini, disappeared on me a couple weeks back."

"He really was Houdini!" Helen laughed.

"I still think I'll wake up one morning with him in my bed. He'll be back when I least expect him."

"In the meantime, I think ye still owe me a dance."

Bill crossed his arms and leaned against the doorframe. "And when would I be able to take you up on that offer?"

"How about this afternoon at Thanksgivin' dinner? We always put on music and dance on big holidays. We have some other guests comin', too...me Aunt Nellie...Mary's husband...Bridie's almost beau."

"I was planning on seeing some buddies early this afternoon—"

"I assumed ye had other plans. Have a wonderful holi—"

"Miss Helen, I was saying I'm seeing them early this afternoon, but I would love to come later."

Helen realized she had been holding her breath. She let out a deep sigh that trailed into an embarrassed giggle.

"Come by any time after three o'clock. Dinner should be ready at four, but first I must get home and give this to Anna. Otherwise, there won't be a dinner," she said, holding up the sugar.

Bill looked up the block in the direction of the Galvin home. "I look forward to it, Miss Helen. Now I won't keep you any longer!"

"Brush up on the Walls of Limerick! We don't make mistakes in me household!" she called, waving as she continued down the street.

"Just you wait, Miss Helen!"

Helen smiled and waved one last time, then picked up her pace, the flutters in her heart fueling her for the last three blocks to home. Bill Rush was coming to Thanksgiving. He was going to dance with her finally. Anna, Mary, and Bridie would get to meet the man who insisted on walking her and Theresa home for protection. Bill Rush was coming, and she couldn't stop smiling. Her cheeks hurt more than her feet from running in heels.

Home came into sight. She ran faster. Anna needed the sugar and Helen needed to sit down. Reaching for the handrail, she pulled herself forward to round the corner onto the stairs. Her foot caught on the bottom stair and she fell forward, dropping the sugar. The bag split and sugar spilled all over the stairs.

"Bloody fuck!" Helen yelled.

She immediately covered her mouth.

Bridie opened the front door as Helen sat there, trying to understand what happened and how that language could have possibly escaped her mouth. She looked up at Bridie, whose own mouth opened wide enough to fit the whole chicken Anna was cooking.

Theresa and Mary came up behind; Theresa with dazed expressions, eyes narrowed and brows slightly knitted together.

"Did ye just say what I think ye did?" Mary asked, tilting her head.

"She sure did. I heard it as I was passin' by to go upstairs," Bridie said.

"The whole street probably heard the obscenity," Theresa added.

Helen didn't even know what to say. What if another *bloody fuck* fell out of her mouth? Now the language was branded in her thoughts. She needed to go to Confession right away. If praying a month's worth of prayers in twenty-four hours didn't work, she could also drink some holy water and swish it around for a long five minutes. Anna would say it was sacrilegious, but she had just said a combination of words that would put Mother and Father in their graves across the Atlantic. She was desperate.

"What's everyone gathered around the front door for? Has Helen returned yet with the sugar?" Anna called as she walked from the kitchen.

When she reached the front door and peered between Mary and Theresa at the mess on the stairs, Anna threw both hands to her forehead and looked from the spilled sugar to Helen and back to the sugar. Helen expected a string of equally atrocious words to come out of Anna's mouth, ordering her to get up and go right back to the store.

Anna just laughed—a deep, hip-bending, snort-escaping belly laugh. A laugh none of the sisters had ever heard.

One by one, Theresa, Mary, and Bridie joined in the laughter until it rang in Helen's ears. She hadn't moved, hadn't spoken, hadn't reacted beyond letting two terrible words slip from her tongue.

"Do we have enough money to buy more sugar?" she asked.

Their laughter died down.

Anna turned her ear to Helen. "Do we have enough what?"

"Money. Do we have enough money to buy more sugar?"

"Well, we'll certainly have enough money for sugar if I sell me emerald necklace at the pawn shop." Bridie giggled.

Anna swatted Bridie with the dishrag in her hand. Theresa shook her head and elbowed Bridie in the side. Mary snatched Bridie's cloche off her head and dangled it above.

And then Helen finally laughed. She was home.

ACKNOWLEDGMENTS

———

I am so incredibly grateful for the three women who entrusted me with their family stories. Caye Haneley, Grace O'Neill, and Kay Scanlon, this book would not have been possible without you. Your mothers' spirits are the heart of this novel.

Thank you to my parents, Bridget and Howard Schmidt, for the unwavering support in my two-year journey that took us across the Atlantic twice, and to my sister, Tara, for allowing me the time to write during quarantine when I could've been with her.

My sincerest thanks to Eric Koester for giving me the once-in-a-lifetime opportunity to write a book at twenty-three years old, and to my dedicated editors, Erika Nichols-Frazer and Rebecca Brunkenstein, for pushing me to craft the best possible version of this book.

Thank you to Elise Most and Amanda Rizkalla for reading the earliest drafts and always reminding me my voice has a place in this world. Thank you to Maya McLeroy and Mollie Brown for being the brightest lights.

I am blessed with an enormous cheer squad as my family. Thank you especially to Edward Rush, Kaitlin Rush, Ginny Minehart, Jamee Rush, Shawn Rush, Beth Puglia,

Mary Farrington, Gavin McBrien, Kristy Farrington, Susan McBrien, Dan Rush, Jen McBrien, Kelly Ethevenin, Susan Adams, Dan Torsiello, Janet Torsiello, and Tracy Ehresman.

To my Stanford friends and peers, I have never met more caring and supportive people. For this book to be born in a creative writing class and finished sitting in my apartment in Phoenix, I never would've made the time to put words on the page without you. Thank you to Sunny Wu, Alanna Simao, Jackie O'Neil, Amy Ma, Melina Walling, Alexis Ivec, Jeffrey Valdespino, Raina Kolluri, Anjini Karthik, Ben Leroy, Jenna Garden, Josh Cobler, Ada Zhou, McKinley McQuaide, Sophie McNulty, Grant Coalmer, Fedra Pouideh, Disha Dasgupta, Kayley Miller, Courtney Douglas, Mailo Numazu, Cynthia Badiey, Lydia Tan, John Barton, Tony Rodriguez, Evan Long, Emma Abdullah, Casey Mullins, Lark Wang, and Leslie Cook.

I am indebted to the teachers who have molded me into a writer and cultivated my creativity from the time I learned to read. Thank you to Dana Beck, Patricia O'Connell, Sue Saddlemire, Rose Cattani, Dawn Nangle, Joy Vander Vliet, Darlene Muldowney, Diana Morris-Bauer, Jen West, Nancy Napoli, Laura Goode, Chris Drangle, and Ximena Briceño.

To my wonderful little Newtown community, I am grateful for the ability to leave home for four years only to return for a visit with open arms. Thank you to Alexandra Gallagher, Kim Galing, Ryan Conner, Nicole Baker, Charissa Stone, Eirene Lo, Susan Spreitzer, Jennifer Voutsinas, Blake Salzman, Julie Lambert, Bridgitte Hogan-Perry, Becca Segel, Christy Cojerian, Margaret Healy, Sara Hibbitts, Maria Rounsavill, Kerry Ledbetter, Courtney Malley, Katherine Ball-Weir, Yasasvi Hari, Min Son, and Bridget O'Malley.

To my family friends, you're supporting not only me but also my mom and grandad. Thank you to Jamie Martin, Kelli Chioffe, Winnie Koebert, Susan Michelson, Lauren Spiece, Karyn Kelly, Joan Travis, Maureen Mehaffey, Denise Holland, Kathy Werley, Joseph Arsenault, Christopher Ruhnke, Lizabeth Cutler, Carol Boland, Lori Hyden, Patti Brown, Alice Chow, Jessica Bishof, Ann Godiksen, Caitlin Brown, Muffy Farrell, Kathleen Cleary, Nancy Boland, and Donna Brown.

Writing this novel has only enriched my love for Irish community that began with ten wonderful years at Rince Ri School of Irish Dance. Thank you to Olivia Hilpl, Dee Adams, Noreen Northrop, Cathleen Lynsky, Annette Baird, Mary Timmins Schluth, Debbie Grant, Melissa Matthews, Ann English, Susan Schmauder, and Jeff Meade.

Thank you to my new Cronkite colleagues who saw my book announcements before they even met me and yet decided to support me: Gianluca D'Elia, Emily Carman, and Michael McDaniel.

Finally, to those I have never met personally, thank you for taking a chance on me. I never would've expected so much love for the Galvin sisters. Thank you to Erin Plante, Kelly O'Connor, Mary Murtagh, Maryann Hurst Kelly, Bernadette Mahr, Katie Rogers, Mollye Rhea, Anne Marie O'Connell, Alanna Barry McCloskey, Rosaleen Rotondi, Eileen O'Rourke, Edward Gillespie, Stacey Polakowski, Hugh McHugh, Kathleen McGirr, Bill Maguire, Mike Maguire, Theresa Garvin, Kelly Burdick, Maureen Clancy, Timothy Garvin, Ann Marie O'Connell, Grace Cavanagh, Archie McGowan, Ronessa McGowan, Bridget Storm, Kelly McGowan, Denise Hilpl, Lisa Maloney, Anne Gavaghan, Lauren O'Neil, Lori Murphy, Janet Wittmer, Niki Chinamanthur, Attracta O'Malley, Rosaleen Megonegal, and William Whitman.

The most important thank-you belongs to the Galvin girls themselves: Anna, Mary, Helen, Theresa, and Bridie. I wish I could've known your struggles and triumphs firsthand, but I hope I did your stories even just a small bit of justice.

Grá go Deo.

APPENDIX

———

AUTHOR'S NOTE

Boland, Eavan. "The Emigrant Irish." Favorite Poem Project. Accessed August 16, 2020. http://www.favoritepoem.org/ poem_TheEmigrantIrish.html.

Kochhar, Rakesh. "Hispanic Women, Immigrants, Young Adults, Those with Less Education Hit Hardest by COVID-19 Job Losses." Pew Research Center. Last modified June 9, 2020. Accessed August 17, 2020. https://www.pewresearch.org/fact-tank/2020/06/09/hispanic-women-immigrants-young-adults-those-with-less-education-hit-hardest-by-covid-19-job-losses/.

"The Impact of COVID-19 on Job Loss: Quick Take." Catalyst. Last modified July 22, 2020. Accessed August 16, 2020. https://www.catalyst.org/research/covid-19-job-loss/.

Tippett, Rebecca. "US Immigration Flows, 1820–2013." Carolina Demography. April 27, 2015. Accessed May 3, 2020. https://www.ncdemography.org/2015/04/27/u-s-immigration-flows-1820-2013/.

US Department of Homeland Security. *Total Immigrants from each Region and Country, by Decade, 1820–2010*. Distributed by Scholastic Corporation. Accessed August 30, 2020. http://teacher.scholastic.com/activities/immigration/pdfs/by_region/region_table.pdf.